RANDOM
ACTS
OF SCROOGE

*A Holly Anna Paladin
Christmas Novella*
(Book 3.5)

By Christy Barritt

RANDOM ACTS OF SCROOGE

CHRISTY BARRITT

RANDOM ACTS OF SCROOGE
By Christy Barritt

Copyright 2015 by Christy Barritt

Published by River Heights Press

Cover design by The Killion Group

RANDOM ACTS OF SCROOGE

CHAPTER 1

I finished placing the last string of garland on my front porch, and I stepped back to admire my hard work. The evergreen twisted with white Christmas lights mirrored the bright stars overhead. The whole scene reminded me of a Christmas card.

Chase had helped my mom and me decorate for Christmas. My family liked to go all out. We had three Christmas trees every year—one in the formal living room, one in the everyday living room, and one in the office. We were late this year in getting the decorations up, but life had been incredibly busy.

I firmly believed that Christmas decorations weren't meant to be rushed or to be put up without thought or pleasure. They were meant to be enjoyed. The process was a time for memories to be indulged in, and, most of all, for the true reason for the season to be celebrated.

Chase's hand slipped around my waist. "I think we did a good job."

I nodded, coming back to the moment. "I'm inclined to agree. I'm feeling very . . . Christmas-y at the moment. What do you say we grab some peppermint hot chocolate and listen to Bing crooning about a white Christmas?" My breath puffed into white frosty air in front of me.

Chase grinned. "I say that's a great idea. Do you think your mom wants to join us?"

"Probably not. She's writing her Christmas cards. But maybe we can make some sugar cookies."

"If that would make you happy."

"And we can look on Pinterest and find some kind of craft. We can make ornaments this year." The ideas exploded in my head and rippled out with excitement. I loved all of the Christmas traditions. Loved them. In my defense, I came from a long line of people who went crazy over the holiday. My uncle and aunt even set up acres upon acres of Christmas displays at their home in West Virginia that people came from all over the state to see.

"You really trust me with a glue gun and glitter?" Chase asked.

Chase hadn't had the chance to experience a Paladin family Christmas yet. Boy, was he in for a treat this year.

"Glue guns and jingle bells and red ribbons—I think you'll handle them all just fine," I told him. I put my gloved hand in his, ready to indulge.

We'd only taken one step toward the house when I heard a car door slam behind me. I turned and saw my neighbor, Mrs. Signet, trudging toward the sidewalk. At the sight of her, a bit of my jolly disappeared.

Something was wrong.

Mrs. Signet's shoulders sagged, and, I couldn't be sure, but her eyes appeared red like she'd been crying. Her hair, which was usually a delicate blonde poof that strangely mimicked her physical build, hung lopsided.

I paused, unable to let the image go. I hated to see people hurting. It was my kryptonite, I supposed.

I excused myself from Chase and started toward her, pulling my red scarf more snuggly around my neck as a brisk wind swept across the lawn. Christmas was only two weeks away, and the weather felt every bit like December should in Cincinnati: cold and brisk. There was no snow—not yet, at least, but I hoped we might get some soon.

"Mrs. Signet, are you okay?" Her family had experienced more than their share of heartaches lately, and I'd been making an effort to check on her as often as I could. She was in her late sixties and had been a widow for probably fifteen years. Living alone was a struggle for her at times.

She dabbed her eyes with a well-used tissue that had been balled in her hands and shook her head. "No, nothing is right. I just got back from visiting my daughter. It's a mess, Holly." Her voice sounded soft and scratchy with age.

I held my breath, waiting to hear what she would say. Her daughter and son-in-law had been in a car accident a few months ago. Both were recovering, but the debt they'd incurred afterward was pushing them toward bankruptcy. I knew they were on the verge of losing their home, and collection agencies were haunting them like the spirits of Christmas Past, Present, and Future.

Someone had started a campaign to raise money to help offset the costs, but I understood it was a long road ahead.

"What's wrong? Is your daughter okay?" I instinctively reached out for Mrs. Signet and squeezed her arm. It felt bonier than I remembered. Had Mrs. Signet been eating enough lately? I needed to bring her more meals and less cakes, I decided. I mentally added that to my checklist.

Chase came to stand behind me. I could feel his body heat emanating from beneath his leather jacket and jeans. It made me want to snuggle up to him and get cozy. He still vaguely smelled of evergreen, and I wanted to lean closer and take in a deep whiff of the scent. But I had other more important matters at hand right now.

"The canisters have been stolen." Mrs. Signet shook her head like that was the most terrible thing in the whole world.

I blinked, her revelation unexpected. "What canisters?"

I imagined heirloom tins of flour and sugar on a kitchen counter. Maybe they were antique and valuable? Maybe they had sentimental significance? I had no idea—I only knew that my neighbor was upset that they'd been stolen.

"The canisters that were left at several of the stores in the area for donations. There was a nice little note attached to them explaining what happened, as well as a picture of Greg and Babette." Mrs. Signet shook her head. "Someone stole three of them. We're guessing there was close to a thousand dollars inside."

"Wow. I'm so sorry." I shook my head in disbelief. "How could someone do this? It's the most un-Christmas thing ever. It's like . . . like

Scrooge himself has come to Cincinnati."

"It may not seem like a lot of money to some people, but Greg and Babette really need that cash. Their children have been through so much, but to possibly lose their house at Christmastime . . ." She shook her head. "It just seems like tragedy upon tragedy."

"I agree." I stole a glance at Chase and saw the troubled look on his face. He practically bristled as he brought his hands to his hips and furrowed his eyebrows.

"Did you call the police about the matter?" he asked.

Mrs. Signet nodded. "We did. Well, the storeowners did. The police made it sound like there wasn't much they could do. I know there are killers on the loose and more serious offenses to pursue. But that money was going to make a difference to one family, and that one family is important to me."

"Every family is important," I assured her, some kind of mama bear instincts rising in me.

My heart ached with compassion. Greg and Babette Sullivan had four children: seventeen, fifteen, thirteen, and nine years old. It had been hard enough on the kids to see their parents in the hospital, but now to have to deal with this . . .

Someone should be very ashamed of themselves for doing such a thing.

"We'll get that money back for you, Mrs. Signet," I announced, determination solidifying in my gut. I raised my chin higher and subtly rolled my shoulders back in somewhat of a Supergirl pose.

Her eyes brightened. "Would you, Sweetie? That would mean the world to us. I just don't know if I can handle much more stress. This old heart isn't the best anymore. My doctor keeps warning me to take it easy."

"I'd be more than happy to help."

"You're such a dear." She patted my hand. "Now I'm going to get inside and sit down for a minute. Here's Bryan's number. He's Greg's cousin, and he's overseeing the fundraising efforts. He'll be happy to talk to you."

"Can I just talk to Babette?"

"They had to cut back on their expenses, so they got rid of their phones." Mrs. Signet let out a sad sigh. "I'm just so heartbroken over this, I don't know what to do."

I took the number and shoved it in the pocket of my white wool coat as Chase walked Mrs. Signet up the steps and into her home. When he joined me again on the sidewalk, he had a far-off look in his eyes. I stepped in front of him and waved my hand in front of his face, pulling him out of his daze.

"It sounds like things have been really rough on them," Chase said. "I know how hard the holidays can be when you're struggling."

Chase had a difficult upbringing. His mom died when he was young, and his dad had never been much of a father. Chase had largely been on his own. I imagined he hadn't had very many happy Christmases, but I was determined to change that this year.

"All these years I've just wanted a normal Christmas, the kind you see on those cheesy Hallmark movies."

"Cheesy?"

He half-shrugged. "They're not exactly guy flicks."

"I concur. I'm hoping you'll have a cheesy— and happy—Christmas this year."

He smiled down at me. "With you, I'm sure I will."

"But first I've got to help Greg and Babette."

"How did I know you were going to get involved in this?" Chase's eyes sparkled.

I shrugged, purposefully overdoing an innocent persona. "Beats me. It's so unlike me to stick my nose in other people's business."

He stepped closer, still glowering down at me because he knew good and well my words weren't true. Shivers rippled through me at his nearness. Nearly a year of dating, and he still made me feel giddy.

"It's exactly like you to see someone who needs help and jump in with both feet." He rested his hands on my waist and pulled me toward him.

"It's like I can't help myself." I tapped my chin, as if the concept stupefied me.

"I'll help you try and figure out what happened," he offered.

My eyebrows shot up. Chase usually encouraged me to stay out of things like this, but he must have thought stolen donation canisters would be safe enough for me to investigate. I'd gotten myself into too many pickles where I'd almost been killed. I had a knack for it, apparently.

"You'll help?"

He shrugged, like it was no big deal. "It's Christmas. Why not do something that will bring good cheer on my time off? Besides, Mrs. Signet is right—everyone's super busy at the station right now. We've had three murders in this area in the past ten days, plus two bank robberies, and four houses that have been broken into. It's not that we don't care. It's just that we're understaffed and only have so many hours in our day."

"You're going to help me?" I repeated, surprise still rippling through me.

"Of course, I'll help." He let out a warm chuckle that sent another burst of shudders down my spine.

"That's the spirit!" I reached on my tippy toes and planted a quick kiss on his lips. "Now, let's go call Bryan. We don't have any time to waste."

CHAPTER 2

Twenty minutes later, I hung up with Bryan Sullivan and turned to Chase. I'd written a page full of notes while sitting at the dining room table and chatting on the phone with him. Chase had kindly made me some coffee and explained to my mother what was going on as I gathered information.

Despite my change of plans, I'd still managed to get in a few of my holiday favorites. Bing crooned in the background, Christmas lights blinked on a tree in the other room, and the whole house smelled like cinnamon from the snickerdoodles I'd made earlier.

Chase munched on one now. He always complained he was going to gain twenty pounds from dating me and all the baking I did. Sugary treats were like fairy dust—they always made people feel better. That's why I often found myself in the kitchen.

"I have a list of the places the canisters were left and which ones were stolen," I announced, raising my steaming coffee mug. "We can go talk to the storeowners and see what we can find out. The money was all stolen earlier today, and I have to guess the canisters were taken by the same person. I mean, what are the odds they weren't?"

Chase sat across from me, his frame making the table look small and dainty. He took a sip of his coffee. He'd found the biggest mug we owned—it looked like a tree trunk. Someone had given it to my dad before he passed away.

"What's strange is, if that's true, someone was specifically targeting this family," Chase said. "Why would they do that? Why would some target a family who's already suffered so much?"

I started to respond when he raised his hand.

"I don't really want an answer," he said. "Believe me. I've seen the depravity of the human soul. Sometimes things just surprise me, though."

"We'll never have any answers if we don't start by asking questions, right?"

He reached across the table and squeezed my hand. "Maybe you should have been a detective, Holly."

I smiled. "Can you really imagine me going through the police academy? Besides, I couldn't wear all of these great dresses if I was a cop."

It wasn't that I was prissy. Not really. I just loved dressing up and fixing my hair and makeup. I liked to feel like a lady. I always told people I was born in the wrong era. It wasn't that things were perfect back in the 1950s, but they'd certainly seemed simpler. The pace of life today, the overwhelming distractions, the ease of abandoning relationships in favor of electronics . . . well, all of that bothered me.

Another reason I couldn't ever become a cop was that I also wasn't very athletic, and the one time I'd punched someone—that someone being a bad guy, at that—I'd felt guilty about it for weeks. No, I'd make a terrible cop.

"I probably wouldn't be able to sleep at night if I thought you were out on the streets seeing some of the things I've seen," Chase said, lowering his voice. I knew he worried about me, and I appreciated his concern.

"I've seen a lot of those things," I reminded him solemnly. I had been a social worker and witnessed some of the worst sides of society. I'd been in the middle of taking kids away from abusers—often people they considered loved ones. It never got easier. Nor did I want it to. Mourning other people's losses made me human.

"Let's not talk about those things. Let's go do some good deeds instead." He reached for my hand. "Let's go."

***

Ten minutes later we pulled up to a convenience store located down the street. I lived in an area called Price Hill. At one time, the neighborhood had been where the upper crust lived. But it had gone downhill as those upper crust moved out into the suburbs and the poor had moved in.

I still thought the place was a treasure, even though it was a shell of what it had once been. But beneath that shell were stories of a time when life here was grander, cleaner, maybe even prettier. The people who lived here now were no less worthy. They just had different kinds of stories to share.

"Could we speak to the store owner, please?" Chase flashed his badge. The teenager behind the counter nodded and disappeared into the back. A moment later, a man of Indian descent emerged. He was probably fifty-something, and he smelled faintly of curry.

"I am Amar Kumar. How can I help you, Detective?" His words sound clipped and tight, broken from the cultural divide between his home country and the new life he'd forged.

"I'm looking for some information about the donation canister that was stolen from your store earlier today."

Amar frowned. "I am sorry to report that is true. It was here one moment, and the next it was gone. No one saw anything."

"Do you have security footage?" I asked.

The man looked me up and down as if trying to surmise if I was Chase's partner. I supposed my red dress and knee-high black boots didn't look too professional. Not for a cop, at least. The man finally turned his nose up at me and looked back at Chase.

"Yes, I do have cameras. But I have not had time to review any footage. Sorry—I have been short-staffed. If I do not maintain my business, people will be setting out donations canisters for me."

"Can we take a look at that footage?" Chase asked.

"Yes, of course." Amar waved. "Follow me. Excuse my office."

The scent of sewage and something else I couldn't identify wafted through my senses as we entered the dark, dirty office located right beside a nasty-looking public restroom.

Papers and trash were everywhere. Calendars, sales reports, and memos were taped to the walls. Half-eaten chips, peanuts, and tubs of food were scattered about.

My stomach turned with revulsion.

For a moment—and just a moment—I was tempted to clean up while Chase found the proper spot in the video footage. However, I didn't think Amar would appreciate it if I rearranged his paperwork. But the temptation was strong. Very strong.

"Don't do it, Holly," Chase muttered after Amar left us alone.

I blinked innocently. "Do what?"

"Try to make his life better by interfering with his disorganized organization system."

I mentally snapped my fingers in an "oh, shucks" moment. Chase knew me all too well. "Clean spaces can make a person feel so much better—"

"Holly . . ."

I raised my hands. "Of course, I'll be good."

Good deeds *had* almost gotten me killed before. One would think I'd have learned my lesson.

Instead of developing a housekeeping plan

for the man, I went to the other side of the desk and leaned over Chase's shoulder, watching as the video footage scrolled by. It was hard to even tell what we were looking at as the images scrambled by in fast-forward. This could take a while.

"You're very . . . distracting," Chase said, pausing for a moment and clearing his throat.

I had no idea what he was talking about. "How so?"

"I find it hard to concentrate sometimes when you're around," he admitted. "Your perfume . . . it's nice."

"I can back up." I secretly glowed under his compliment.

He grabbed my hand and kept me close. "No, I'll be good. I'm just used to working with stinky old men."

I was finding it hard to concentrate myself at the moment. I stared at the TV screen instead, ignoring my rush of attraction toward Chase. "Right there! Look."

Chase rewound the footage, and we watched as a man came to the counter wearing a large coat. A hat was pulled down low over his face, and he averted his gaze from the camera, almost like he knew it was there. He checked out, the clerk gave him a paper bag with some soda and a bag of chips in it. Then, ever so subtly, the man, as he grabbed his bag, also swept up the donation canister into his arms.

The clerk—the same teenager who was out there now—looked like he'd rather be anywhere else than working. He'd barely looked at the man or spoken to him, if I was interpreting the video correctly.

Customer service these days . . . it wasn't what it used to be. Of course, most things weren't.

"Let me see if I can print a picture of this guy." Chase shook his head as he stared at the screen. "The angle doesn't offer very much."

I stared at the man's image on the monitor. "I agree. I'm just guessing, but I'd say the guy is in his mid-to-late twenties. He's white, relatively thin, and he likes the Reds, which rules out—well, it rules out almost no one here in Cincinnati."

"He's smooth." Chase narrowed his eyes as he studied the footage. "It's almost like he rehearsed taking the canister."

"He's wearing a leather jacket. At least, that's how it looks. He certainly doesn't appear poor."

"Many people wear expensive clothing. That tells nothing about their social economic status in today's society. Besides, it could be pleather."

I nibbled on my lip. "That's true. What do we do now?"

"We print this picture, and then we visit the other stores. We need to figure out first if this is the same guy. Then we go from there."

**

Two hours later, we had confirmed it was indeed the same guy. At each location, the thief had carefully averted his face from the cameras. One store even had a camera in the parking lot, but the man had managed to keep his head down and his face out of sight there also.

Chase and I had concluded the man hadn't driven to each of the stores. He'd gone around the corner at one location to an area covered by grass. An apartment complex sat on the other side surrounded by streets upon streets of houses.

I looked up at Chase as we climbed into his Jeep. "What now?"

"The options are limited, Holly. No one recognized the man, we have no license plate, and the pictures are grainy, not to mention the man kept his face concealed. This is going to be a tough one to crack."

"Can't we mark the locations on a map and then find the center point which will clearly indicate the area where the man might live—"

"Maybe in the movies," Chase said. "Even if that was correct, in this case, it would be a matter of going door-to-door and asking people if they recognize him. That takes a lot of man power and time."

I frowned. "There's got to be something we can do."

"I do have one idea. We can go to the stores where the remaining canisters are. We'll leave a photo of the man and ask the employees to call us if the guy comes in. If the clerk can stall the suspect, maybe we can get there in time to catch the man."

"Brilliant plan." I nodded, finally satisfied that we were doing something. But there was more. "I have an idea also."

"What's that?"

"I'm going to plan an even better fundraiser to collect money for the family. We'll blow these canister donations out of the water. And I'll set up an online campaign also. I mean, really, that's what most people do nowadays. The time of canisters in convenience stores is about a decade late."

"It sounds like we have some work to do."

I nodded. "Yes, we do!"

It was time to prove to Scrooge that he couldn't ruin Christmas . . . not if Holly Anna Paladin had anything to do with it.

CHAPTER 3

"All right, everyone. How are those Christmas Croissants coming?" I called, observing my work crew as they scurried around the kitchen. There were probably twenty people here, and each had been assigned a different task.

"Just great, Ms. Holly," Heidi said.

"Wonderful. How about the Polar Pancakes?" I continued, pacing like a drill sergeant at boot camp. Only I was pacing an inner-city kitchen, and the youth there were helping me with the task at hand. The females were, at least. The guys had disappeared outside to play basketball with the center's director, Abraham.

"Polar Pancakes are right on target!"

"Fabulous. The Fa La La La Fudge?" I wiped some flour from my Ms. Claus apron. I'd been giving impromptu baking lessons and having a great time getting down and dirty in the kitchen.

"It's yummy!" Katrina popped a piece in her mouth and closed her eyes with delight.

I playfully took my wooden spoon and tapped her hand. "No snitching. But it is good, isn't it?"

She nodded with wide, satisfied eyes. "It's delicious."

I cleared my expression, trying to look more serious than I felt. "Christmas Tree Bark?"

"It's to die for," Tana said.

I nodded, feeling satisfied. "Great. I appreciate you all coming together for the cause."

In my defense, I'd not only recruited teens from the youth center, but I'd also brought in some of my coworkers from my brother's office. Ralph was a state senator, and the staff was always looking for causes to join in together. I'd unofficially become the instigator of such things. Thankfully, Ralph let us have two hours of volunteer time every week, so I had a work force that was more than willing to leave the office for a little while.

Because I wasn't actually all business, I'd brought in some sandwiches, cookies, and cinnamon-covered popcorn for my volunteers. I blared Christmas music in the background—"Run, Run, Rudolph" played right now—and I'd purchased some cheap Santa hats for people to wear. I'd done my best to turn this into a party. I'd also been sure to remind people that volunteer hours looked great on college applications.

My best friend, Jamie Duke, was also here making gluten-free selections out of almond flour, coconut flour, oat fiber, and every other wheat alternative she could find. I'd used some money from my secret reserve to buy all the ingredients we needed. I used my "stash of cash" to help with various needs in the community whenever I saw fit. It was one of the advantages to living at home—I had some extra money.

Tomorrow we were having a bake sale. A whole block in downtown Cincinnati would be closed for the city's annual Christmas bazaar, which featured various vendors. Ralph had pitched in for the table space and secured an area near his office.

I hoped hoards of people would be out Christmas shopping. The event was a sleighload of fun. Santa would be walking around, carolers and apple cider would be abundant, and a wonderful selection of homemade goods like soap, jam, dips, birdhouses, jewelry, and everything else imaginable would be available for purchase. I could hardly wait.

All money we raised would go toward Greg and Babette. Maybe—hopefully—this would make up for the money that was stolen from them.

"Jamie, have you got this under control here?" I took off my apron and handed it to one of the teens.

My BFF nodded, proceeding to do a Z-shaped finger snap that ended with her hand on her hip. "You know it, girlfriend. I was born to be a control freak. Where are you headed again?"

"I've got to meet with Greg, Babette, and Bryan. I want to find out what the exact need is."

One of my coworkers was one of, if not the, smartest PR people in the state. She'd agreed to help me, and I was already mentally drafting news releases and forming a media campaign for this. But I needed more information first.

"I've got this," Jamie continued, taking away my wooden spoon and slapping it in her hand. "If there's one thing my momma taught me it's how to be a bossy britches."

"Make Mama Val proud then." I grabbed my keys and paused for a moment, considering my words. "But these are volunteers, so make sure their day remains merry and bright."

"Oh, ye of little faith. It's the most wonderful time of the year. Of course I'll be nice."

***

Fifteen minutes later, I pulled up to a small house located on the east side of town, not too far from Price Hill, where I lived. This particular section was especially rundown and dirty, and some shady looking characters lounged on the sidewalk.

I quickly skirted by them and knocked on the door to Greg and Babette Sullivan's place. A moment later, Babette answered.

Growing up, I had known Babette, but she was at least fifteen years older than me. Though the age difference between us wasn't huge as adults, I'd always think of her as being significantly older since she was a teenager while I learned to walk.

Babette was close to six feet tall and had probably been considered big-boned as a child. Time and age had not been kind to her, making her chin nearly disappear and fat collect in her abdomen. Her hair was blonde like her mom's, but it came down to her shoulders in stringy waves.

I greeted her with a hug before nodding at Greg, who sat in a recliner in the background, wearing a neck brace. Another man was there also. He was probably close to my age and had a slouching midsection and sloppy clothes.

"Bryan." He extended his hand. "Nice to put a face with the name."

"Holly."

"Bryan has been living with us . . . I guess as far back as Indiana," Babette explained. "He's practically an adopted son."

I thought it was interesting that people who were barely making it financially were actually supporting someone else. But the gesture also showed kindness.

The tiny house was crammed already, but my presence seemed to overwhelm the minuscule living room. Babette and Bryan crowded onto the couch, Greg remained on the recliner, and I sat on a dining room chair that had been stashed in a corner.

There was no Christmas tree in the house, I realized. I couldn't help but wonder why. If I had an opportunity, I would ask.

My family obviously loved Christmas trees, which was why we had three. My favorite one stood in the every-day living room. It wasn't the pretty tree. No, it had colorful lights and a gaudy garland. It was slightly lopsided, and the branches didn't fill out enough to cover the gaps between them.

What I loved about the tree were the ornaments from my childhood, many of them handmade in grade school and consisting of pompoms, popsicle sticks, and handprints. But the tree also had wooden designs my dad had made. He'd created a new design every year, and we'd given the masterpieces to people at church, neighbors, coworkers, and friends.

My dad had loved to build things out of wood, and looking at those pieces as I'd put them on the tree had been especially bittersweet this year. It had been two years since he passed, and this Christmas wouldn't be any easier than the last one without him. He should be here with us still.

"How are you all doing?" I started, feeling a touch like the social worker I'd once been.

"We're sore, but we're getting there," Babette said. "I'm having a terrible time walking. Greg hurt his neck and should be going to physical therapy, but we've had to reduce our appointments. The bills are more than we can handle."

"Even copays and deductibles can add up after a while," Greg said. "I owned my business and didn't purchase disability insurance. No work means no pay."

"I wondered if you'd been able to go back to the job yet," I said.

"No, I own a plaster business, but I can't work with my neck like this."

32

"It's too bad because he's one of the best in the area, and we've had to turn down several jobs," Babette said. "I'm hoping they'll save my job for me at B-Mart, but I've missed so much time. Who knows?"

I frowned as the reality of their struggle became even more apparent. "Well, I don't want to take up too much of your time. I was hoping to get some more information about what's happening. Obviously, I talked to Bryan last night and he told me about the fundraising efforts. But I stopped by so I could hear about you two—beyond the fundraising. Your mom already told me you're afraid of losing your house, and I know no one wants to see that happen. You've already been through enough."

"Thank you," Babette said. "We don't want to lose this place either. Unfortunately, we were already behind on payments before the accident thanks to some of Greg's clients who didn't pay him like they were supposed to. We thought we'd be able to get caught up . . . then all of this happened. I know we could live with Mom, but it would be hard on her with all the kids there. I don't want to put any more stress on her—not with her heart and all."

She had a good point. Mrs. Signet's house

would be tight, and the older woman valued her routine and privacy. "Tell me what happened."

"We were coming back from buying groceries. A car ran a red light and T-boned us. Larry Jenkins—he was the other driver and, unfortunately, his name will forever be burned into my mind—he claimed that *we* were the ones who ran the light. There were no cameras to verify either side. Thanks to two witnesses, we ended up being cited for the accident. It's a mess. Adding even more strain to the whole situation is that he's bringing a civil suit against us to try to get more money for the time he lost from work."

I shifted, hating to ask the uncomfortable questions, but I wouldn't do anyone any favors by remaining silent. "If you don't mind me asking, what kind of bills are we talking about?"

"They keep coming in. Just when we think they're done, a new one arrives in our mailbox. Even with insurance, the costs are unbelievable." Babette stretched her leg and cringed with each motion.

Greg spoke up. "What she's not telling you is that our bills are already over twenty thousand dollars. I expect more to come. We spent ten days in the hospital, plus we have ongoing therapy."

Twenty thousand dollars? I couldn't begin

to imagine.

"Wow. I'm so sorry." I shifted as I thought the situation through. "So, obviously Bryan stepped up to help. I don't want to intrude in anyone else's territory."

"I can use all the help I can get," Bryan said. "I deliver packages for a living, so I have no experience with things of this nature. I just knew that someone had to do something. Greg and Babette don't deserve any of this. They've been generous enough to let me stay here with them until I can get back on my feet. No one thought the tables would turn like this."

"He's been such a help," Babette added. "I don't know what we would have done without him. He's almost like an older brother to the kids. Even though he has the money to venture out on his own now, he's stayed here out of the goodness of his heart. He's like our family angel."

Bryan shook his head. "She speaks too highly of me. I'm just doing what any decent human would. I decided to set up the canisters because I remembered someone did something like that for a lady at work several years ago and ended up raising almost six hundred dollars. I thought it would be a start."

I nodded, not feeling very optimistic about

his plan but keeping my thoughts silent. There was no need of insulting someone who was trying to do good work. "How would you feel about going broader with these efforts? Maybe even taking your story to the media?"

Babette shook her head quickly and adamantly. "I don't know about that. I don't really like attention."

"But attention can bring support, and support can bring funds you need," I told her.

She frowned. "Maybe as a last resort. I really don't have the look for TV anyway. Plus, you go public, and everyone begins scrutinizing you. I don't know if I can handle that. I have enough to deal with."

I didn't push any more. I wanted to help them, not make them uncomfortable, and media attention was a personal choice. "That's understandable. Let me see what I can do. I'd like to set up a profile for you on one of the online sites where people can make donations. How would you feel about that?"

"We'll take all the help we can get. We really appreciate you doing this for us, Holly. We'd lost hope until Mom told us you wanted to help."

I forced a smile. I did want to help. I only prayed my efforts worked because otherwise Greg and Babette's hopes would be dashed. I didn't want that to happen. Especially since I was the one who would be responsible.

"By the way, are you decorating for Christmas this year?" I asked as I stood, hoping I sounded casual enough.

Babette shook her head. "I just don't have the energy. Besides, we threw our old artificial tree away last year since half of the branches were broken. We never anticipated this happening."

Just then my phone rang, and I saw that it was Chase. I excused myself to answer.

"Holly, I'm heading over to Circle Express on Eighth Street. An employee thinks our guy might be there."

My pulse spiked. "I'll meet you."

"Don't approach him until I get there. Not even then, for that matter. You promise?"

"Of course. I'll be on my best behavior."

"Holly . . ."

I twisted my lips in a frown. "I promise. If for no other reason than I'd hate to make Santa's naughty list."

CHAPTER 4

Chase beat me to the Circle Express. By the time I pulled up, he was already outside and talking to a man wearing a Reds cap. I observed them for a moment while I sat in my warm 64 ½ powder-blue classic Mustang. Chase, wearing a gray sweater with a thick collar and black pants, didn't seem too on edge as he talked to the man.

I observed the suspect carefully. It could be him, I supposed. He was about the same height and build. Something about the way he carried himself seemed different from the man in the video, though. He almost seemed more cultured or confident.

I climbed out and joined them in front of the store, just in time to hear part of their conversation.

"I have no idea what you're talking about. I just came in here planning to buy some milk and cookies." The man frowned. "Well, I only planned on buying the milk. I was going to eat the cookies before I got home and my wife saw them."

"A man matching your description has been stealing donation jars around town," Chase said.

The man pointed to himself and laughed. "You think I'm going to steal someone's charity? I may not be the wealthiest man in the city, but I am an engineer. I make more than enough money, and I don't need to steal anyone else's cash. Especially not at Christmas."

Chase glanced up and nodded at me, an unspoken conversation happening in that brief moment. We both understood that this wasn't our man. He was innocent. This man was dressed nicely. There was only one other car in the parking lot and it was an Acura—not the cheapest brand. And it was well-maintained.

I just couldn't picture this man as the culprit.

"Can I go now?" The man didn't sigh audibly, but I could hear the urge in his voice.

Chase nodded. "Thank you for your time."

As the man climbed into his vehicle, Chase and I remained outside. Brisk winter air assaulted any exposed skin, making me second-guess the cute forest-green dress with the wide black belt. Forecasters said we might have snow flurries this weekend.

"Looks like that lead was a bust," Chase said.

"I can see why the clerk thought it might be him. He fits the description."

"I wish we had a better visual on the man. But we have to work with what we have." We walked slowly, almost hesitantly, toward my car. Were we stretching the conversation out? Trying to delay the inevitable task of returning to life in favor of stealing a few more minutes together?

Why, yes, we were.

"How's your day going?" Chase asked.

"I just finished meeting with Greg and Babette. I also put a small army to work, making goodies for the bake sale and downtown bazaar tomorrow. Do you think you'll be able to stop by?"

"I intend on trying, unless I get pulled away on a big case. I think it's best if we pursue raising more money to make up for what was stolen."

I nodded, familiar heaviness on my chest. "I know you're right. But what about justice?"

"I agree. But the thought I keep coming back to is this: What if the person who stole that money needs it more than Greg and Babette?"

"You and I both know he's probably using it for drugs." I was usually the optimistic one, but I wasn't naïve either. The odds were that this wasn't someone desperate for food. More likely it was someone driven by addictions and compulsions.

"You're probably right. Desperate people do desperate things. Drugs make people desperate." He paused by my car door.

"Besides, I can't imagine that many people who need the money more than Greg and Babette. Their financial burden would overwhelm anyone." My heart felt heavy every time I remembered what they were going through. Life and heartaches seemed to have a proclivity to unabashedly pile on at times.

"Their situation is that bad, huh?"

I nodded, remembering my conversation with Babette. "Already over twenty thousand in bills."

"Wow." Chase rubbed his chin and frowned.

I grabbed my keys and straightened, determination strengthening my resolve. "I will keep focusing on raising money. But I'm not quite ready to let this go, either."

"Where are you headed off to now?"

An idea swirled in the back of my mind, but I wasn't ready to share it yet. I needed to think it through a little more first. "I'm stopping by the youth center to check on the bake-a-thon there.

Then we'll see what else the day holds."

"But no trouble?" He brushed a loop of hair off my shoulder and peered down at me with that warm look in his eyes.

I smiled, confident that I would play it safe. "No trouble."

***

"You're going to be in so much trouble," Jamie muttered.

"We're just paying a visit to Larry Jenkins," I explained to Jamie as we cruised down the road. She'd just finished cleaning up at the youth center, and I owed her big time. "It's no big deal."

"Who is Larry Jenkins again?"

"He's the man who was in the car accident with Greg and Babette."

"Yes, yes . . . of course. And you think he stole the money from Greg and Babette?"

I shrugged, realizing it sounded far-fetched. "I have no idea. I'm collecting information—then I'll draw conclusions."

"Does Chase know you're doing this?"

I frowned as I made my way through the stop-and-go traffic on the overcast day. When I'd left Chase, I was still chewing on the idea of speaking with Larry. I was tempted to go back to the office, but I couldn't go on with life as usual. That wasn't my style.

"I wasn't 100 percent sure I was doing this last time we spoke, so no, he doesn't. But he's busy with other things. Like work."

"Speaking of which, aren't you supposed to be working?"

"Ralph gave me the day off to help organize this bake sale. It's a win-win for him. We help a needy family, and Ralph's staff shows they care about the constituents in the area."

"That doesn't sound like you. It sounds all fakey-fake."

"We do care. *I* care." I shook my head, my grip tightening on the wheel. "Politics are complicated. To say appearances aren't important would be a lie. It's a delicate balance. If I can get people to try out volunteering, I'm convinced they'll become addicted and want to do more of it. It's contagious like that."

"Okay, I get where you're coming from. Now, tell me about this Larry guy."

I leaned back, trying to relax. It was useless. I was entirely too wound up. "Let's see. He's in construction. They're working on building a new apartment complex out in Western Hills."

"How'd you find that out?"

"It was pretty easy. I did an Internet search for Larry, found his profile on social media, and saw what company he worked for. People put everything out there on the Internet for all the world to see. They practically let you know when they go the bathroom. Manners today have gone down the . . . toilet." I swallowed hard at my unintentional word choice.

"Holly, focus here."

"Right, right. Anyway, then I called the company and asked to speak with Larry. The kind woman who answered told me he was working on a building project near the movie theater in Western Hills."

Jamie took a small bottle from her purse and dabbed something peppermint-scented behind her ears. "Essential oil. I feel a cold coming on, and peppermint helps me every time. Anyway, it sounds like you did some good work investigating."

"I had no idea how far I would get. I still don't know, for that matter. This Larry guy could shut up and not say anything. He could be innocent in all of this. Who knows unless we ask questions."

"Asking questions has put us in a bind before, or have you forgotten?"

"I have no idea what you could possibly be

talking about—"

"Let me refresh your memory. There was the time you broke into someone's house and—"

"Never mind." I stopped her before her tabulation became longer than Santa's list of Christmas Eve stops. "Yes, I do remember. Speaking of which, what do you say we break into someone's home and decorate for Christmas?"

Jamie groaned beside me. "You're not serious, are you?"

I flashed a devious smile. "Not really. I mean, I *would* like to ambush the family by showing up with Christmas decorations. But there will be no breaking in involved."

"I guess that could be fun. A great way to spread some holiday cheer. I can't believe I'm saying that."

"Excellent. I'm going to see if I can find someone to donate the tree. I'll keep trying to organize the details." I pulled up to a construction site where a four-story apartment complex would be going in and parked in the paved lot beside it. Several workers were gathered in the distance, looking at something in the center of their huddle. If I had to guess, it was between construction plans or a cute cat video.

"Here goes nothing," Jamie muttered.

We climbed out, and I straightened my dress as we approached the men. My eyes scanned each of them. I'd seen pictures of Larry online, and I knew he was in his early thirties. I couldn't tell that much else about him based on his headshot, though. It was especially challenging to identify him since all the men wore hard hats, tool belts, and safety vests.

The huddle dispersed before we reached them, but one man lingered behind. He was the older one of the bunch, which led me to believe he was in charge.

"Can I help you ladies?" His voice sounded gruff and uninterested. He lowered his clipboard to his side, and his eyes narrowed as he studied us.

"We're looking for Larry Jenkins. We heard he could be here," I said.

His shaggy eyebrows shot in the air. "Larry? Yeah, he's here."

"Could I ask you a couple of questions about Larry?" I rushed. "It's for a . . . surprise."

He paused, his hands going to his hips and his eyes narrowing even farther. "Yeah, I guess. What do you need?"

"We heard he was in a car accident a while ago," I quickly said. "How's he doing?"

The man shrugged. "Fine, I guess. I don't

know."

"We heard it was serious and he had to miss quite a bit of work. I guess it's a good thing he had the money to hire lawyers for that civil suit he has coming up."

"Money?" The man snorted. "Well, I don't know where he got it. Not by working here. Although he did buy a new flat-screen TV a few days ago. Hearing him talk about it, it was pretty nice. Fifty-two-inch, HD. Had some other pretty sweet features. Maybe he's got a sugar mama." He snorted again.

I glanced at Jamie. "Really? You said he just got it? That's interesting."

"Who are you guys, anyway?"

I swallowed hard, trying not to look as uncomfortable as I felt. "We're organizing a fundraiser for . . . people down on their luck this holiday season. A friend of a friend told us about Larry, and we wondered if he was a candidate. I imagine his legal bills have cleaned out his checking account."

"Fundraiser? Really? Well, I suppose if there's ever a time to be generous, it's Christmas. I just didn't expect two sugar-plum fairies to show up." He laughed at himself again, but the sound ended in a coughing fit.

I forced a polite smile.

"Well, I hope he does get some help," the man sobered. "He's had a bad run of luck lately, and if he has much more time off work, he may not have a job."

"I see."

He glanced over his shoulder. "Speaking of the devil, here he comes."

I glanced up. Sure enough, it was Larry from social media. Only, in real life, Larry was rather tall and thin. He also carried himself like someone who was up to no good.

Could *Larry* be stealing money from Greg and Babette?

Maybe I'd just found our man.

CHAPTER 5

"Larry, it's your lucky day," Boss Man said. "You've got Cindy Lou Who and Cindy Lou Two here to see you."

I cast the wannabe comedian a dirty look.

Larry eyed us. "Cindy Lou Who and Two, huh?"

I shuddered again. There was something about this man that seemed off, that made me feel a little scared. Maybe it was his shifty gaze or the way his shoulders hunched. I wasn't sure.

"Apparently they want to give you money." Mr. Hack-Up-a-Lung's words trailed off as he walked away.

Good riddance.

I shifted uncomfortably again before flashing a smile at Larry that I hoped made me look trustworthy. Maybe it was because the Boss Man had planted the idea in my head, but I couldn't help but think that Larry looked a little like the Grinch. He had beady eyes, a disappearing chin, and a stubby little nose.

"You must be Larry," I started.

"And you are?"

"I like to call myself Holly Jolly Christmas." I cringed when I heard myself. Maybe I should have stuck with Cindy Lou Who.

He looked at Jamie. "And you?"

"Joyful Jamie." As soon as the words left her lips, she frowned, standing in stark contrast to her name.

Doubt flashed in Larry's eyes. "And what kind of money is this that you guys want to give me?"

"We're a part of the Christmas Benevolence Fund. We look for people who are down on their luck, and we try to offer them a Christmas wish," I said.

"And you heard about me how?"

"Through a friend of a friend—who wishes to remain anonymous."

"Is that right?" He cocked an arm up on his hip. "This 'friend' thinks I'm down on my luck?"

Something about his words chilled me. I had to continue with my cover, though. "It's Christmas. That's no time for auto accidents and medical bills and lawsuits."

"Isn't that interesting. So you came all the

way out here to find me. That's an awful lot of trouble. Certainly there are other people more worthy of your attention. Who sponsors this Christmas fund?"

"Anonymous donors," I quickly told him.

"Uh huh." He crossed his arms. "What do you want to do for me?"

"Well, first we wanted to find out if you had any needs. We have to screen people before granting wishes."

A glimmer of hunger—a lust for more— glistened in his eyes. "Sure. I always have needs. I need a new job since my back hurts from the accident. Can you help with that? My boss has been giving me a hard time. Just because I've had two accidents in a year doesn't mean they're my fault."

"Jobs are a little harder to come by than financial donations," I told him.

"But maybe you could benefit from some driving lessons," Jamie quipped.

As Larry narrowed his eyes, I shot Jamie a warning glance. She didn't like the man. Neither did I, for that matter. But I still needed more information.

"You're not really from a Christmas fund, are you? You're here to find out information on me. Who are you really working for? The insurance company? Or maybe those Sullivans managed to scrounge up money for a lawyer and you work for them?"

"I don't know why you're getting defensive. Usually only people who are guilty get defensive," I quipped.

"You better watch your tone," he growled. "I'm not letting no little girl get the best of me. I tried to settle this out of court, but those Sullivans claimed they couldn't do it. Said they didn't have any money."

I raised my hand, realizing our time here was done. But he wasn't going to get the best of me, either. "I can see you're not a good candidate for the fund, but maybe you are a good candidate for manners school."

"Manners school?" Venom dripped from his words.

I raised my chin, refusing to break eye contact.

Finally he burst into laughter. "That's just about the funniest thing I've heard all month. Manners school. Maybe I can go to charm school after that. At the end I can be a debutante? My mom would be so proud."

He laughed harder.

Jamie and I used that as an excuse to mosey back to my car. He was still laughing—maniacally, I might add—when we pulled away.

"That was weird." Jamie shivered and rubbed her arms.

"You can say that again. He was creepy. Weird creepy. Like, I don't know if something's seriously wrong with him or if he's just got a twisted sense of humor." I paused. "But he fits the description, Jamie."

"A lot of people around here do," she reminded me.

"I know. But what if he's the one who's been stealing the money? I mean, he has a personal reason to target the family. If he thinks the accident was their fault, then maybe he resents money being raised for them. Maybe he thinks the money is rightfully his."

"I don't put many things past people."

I sighed and shook my head. "I'm not ruling him out. Maybe he's vindictive and wants to hurt them."

"You never know." Jamie sighed. "What next, Holly Jolly Christmas? Or maybe I like Cindy Lou Who better. It kind of fits you."

I shook my head again. "I have no idea, Joyful Jamie. We'll do the bazaar tomorrow and hopefully raise enough money to help the Sullivans out. They need twenty thousand dollars, though. I was hoping to make maybe a thousand. In the big picture, it doesn't seem like that much."

"I'm sure every bit will help."

I nodded. "I know. Speaking of which, I need to go to the youth center and make sure everything is packaged up and ready to go. I've got a lot of work to get done."

"I'll help."

I smiled, grateful for our friendship. "Let's go."

***

The Christmas bazaar was everything I thought it would be. The scent of cinnamon, evergreen, and peppermint filled the air. Carolers—led by Dr. Evans, the choir director from my church—sang in the background, wandering from booth to booth. Everything was decorated in green and red. Even the weather was cooperating. It was overcast and chilly, but there was no snow.

Our bake sale table was hopping. I wasn't sure if it was the free samples we were giving out, the cause, or the scrumptious recipes, but the crowds hadn't stopped coming. Even our fruitcake was selling, but, in its defense, this was no ordinary fruitcake. It was actually good.

Only two hours into the sale, half of our goodies were gone and we'd raised more than one thousand dollars. At least I could rest assured that the same amount of money that was stolen from Greg and Babette would be given back to them. I had plenty of help, including a couple of teens who were able to get in their community service hours and three coworkers were able to volunteer with their families.

I'd invited Greg and Babette to stop by, but so far I hadn't seen them. I had seen people from the office, church, and a couple of acquaintances from the community. The bazaar was a tradition that brought out a lot of locals. I'd bypassed my normal frilly dress in favor of jeans and a thick, red turtleneck sweater, as well as a red scarf and knit hat.

I stepped back from the table a moment to survey the area when I heard a deep voice behind me call my name. I turned and saw Chase standing there, wearing my favorite black sweater and khakis. I quickly reached up and kissed his cheek.

"Hey, Handsome," I murmured. "Fancy seeing you here."

His eyes seemed to glow. "It's always good

to see you."

"Come on. Let me get you something to eat. I made my toffee poke cake. I know how you love that one, so I pulled a piece aside just in case you showed up."

"You always look out for me, don't you?"

"I try." I grabbed a piece of cake from behind the table and handed it to him with flourish. "Just for you."

"Looks fantastic." His gaze scanned the crowds as he unwrapped the cake. "Your treats seem to be selling like hotcakes."

"I can't complain. We've already raised more than a thousand dollars. The Fa La La La Fudge and Christmas Tree Bark have sold out already."

"Excellent news. You never cease to amaze me, Holly. You pulled this together quickly and successfully."

"Only by God's grace." I crossed my arms to fight the breeze. "Any updates on the search for the thief?"

He shook his head and took a bite of the cake. "Nope, not a single one. I did ask a few people if they recognized the man from the security footage while I was in the neighborhood around one of the convenience stores today. No one recognized the picture."

"That's a shame. I went ahead and set up an 'I Need Moola' account online for them. I'm hoping that will bring in more money. The Sullivans aren't interested in any media attention at this point."

"Some people are private like that."

"I know. It would make it easier, though, if I could go public. I had a plan all worked out."

"Mary and Joseph had a plan also, and it didn't go the way they envisioned."

"I can't argue with that. Yet everything worked out anyway, right? A Savior was born, and hope for all became a reality."

"Absolutely."

"Ms. Holly," Tana, one of my youth center girls, called.

"Yes?" I looked over and saw that she looked pale. No customers were nearby giving her a hard time, and everything appeared to be running smoothly.

"We have a problem."

"What's that?" Food poisoning? *Please, no food poisoning.* And we'd properly marked everything with nuts for those who had allergies.

She held up the cashbox. "All our money is missing."

CHAPTER 6

"What do you mean?" I rushed toward her and looked inside the metal box myself. All the bills were gone and only a handful of change remained.

Tana shook her head, tears welling in her eyes. "I have no idea. One minute it was here. I turned to help another customer, and when I came back the cashbox was empty."

"Was anyone watching it?" Ralph was supposed to be here any minute now to take the bulk of the money from us and put it in the safe at his office.

"Tyreese was restocking on the opposite side, and the two ladies from your office took off on their break." She shook her head. "I'm so sorry, Ms. Holly. I have no idea how this happened. I should have never taken my eyes off it."

"Don't beat yourself up," I assured her, even though frustration mounted inside me—not at Tana, but at the person who'd taken the money.

"Tyreese, did you see anything?" Chase

stepped closer.

Chase was beginning to build a relationship with the teens, who in general saw cops as the enemy, by coming out to play basketball at the youth center a couple of nights per week. I hoped he'd be able to make connections with them because peace was desperately needed between the two groups.

Tyreese raised his hands in innocence. "I didn't do anything—except snitch a piece of chocolate peppermint cake. I'll pay for it. I promise."

"I wasn't accusing you, Tyreese. I just wanted to know if you saw anything." Chase dropped his plate in a nearby trashcan.

"Unfortunately, no. Sorry." He shook his head. "Nothing. I was selling some Jingle Bell Crunch when I heard Tana talking to you guys. It's the first I caught wind of it."

I sighed and glanced around, looking for a sign of anyone suspicious. All I saw were crowds sashaying from booth to booth, looking jolly with the holidays.

Who would have stolen the money? Someone was obviously targeting Greg and Babette. I'd known that from the start, but now this person was taking it to the extreme. I couldn't believe he'd be this brazen.

"I'll cover the north side of the bazaar," Chase said.

"I'll head the opposite way," I said before turning to Tana and Tyreese. "You guys watch the booth, okay?"

"You still trust me?" Tana's eyes were still watery as she asked the question.

"You didn't steal the money, did you?"

Tana shook her head.

"Then you did nothing wrong. We'll talk more when I get back. Time is of the essence right now, and I want to search for whoever did this."

I headed down the street, looking for a man in a Reds hat. I didn't have expectations of finding him. But I would kick myself if I didn't look.

I surveyed the area as I rushed down the street, which had been blocked from car traffic. Most people took their time and lingered at booths, leisurely shopping. I kept my eyes open for someone hurrying to get away.

I reached the end of the line of booths and paused. Nothing. No one.

Where had the thief gone? How could someone sink this low?

Irritated, I turned and made my way back to the bake sale. I paused when I saw someone walking toward me.

It couldn't be.

It was.

Larry Jenkins.

He strolled my way, a woman on one arm and several bags dangling from the other. His eyes widened when he saw me charging toward him.

"*You* took that money," I muttered.

"Excuse me?" His eyes narrowed and his stance instantly became defense: shoulders rigid, jaw set, muscles stiff. Recognition flashed across his features. "You again. Cindy Lou Who."

"You took the money I was raising for Greg and Babette Sullivan." I said each word with punch and more guts than I thought I had. "I want it back."

"You're crazy, lady. I thought you were on the Christmas Benevolence Fund. You sound more like a cop right now."

I wouldn't be distracted here. "That money is missing, and you're here. You're the logical suspect."

"Lady, you leave my man alone. He didn't take your money." The woman on his arm raised her chin in a dare-to-defy-me look.

The woman's hair was long and unnaturally black, her skin over-bronzed and orange, and her clothes went beyond tight to too small.

She wasn't going to intimidate me. "Then you won't mind showing me what's in those bags."

"It's none of your business what we bought today," Larry shot back. "Now if you'll excuse me, we'll be on our way."

At that moment, Chase appeared beside me. "Everything okay?"

"This is the man who hit Greg and Babette's car," I said thrusting my finger toward Larry. Pointing was so impolite, but I'd sacrifice my manners for justice.

"Do I need to call the cops on you, lady?" Larry said.

Chase flashed his badge. "I am the cops. Now what's going on?"

"She's harassing me," Larry said. "First, she pretended she wanted to give me money, and now she's accusing me of stealing."

Chase threw me a questioning look before turning back to Larry. I had no doubt he would be asking me about that a little later. Perhaps I should have fessed up about my visit to the construction site when I talked to Chase last night, but it was too late for that now.

"It is quite the coincidence that you're here right when the money was stolen. You also match the description of the person suspected of the store thefts," Chase said.

Larry's lips curled up in a sneer. "That means nothing. My girl and I come here every year for Christmas. Her mama sells crocheted toilet paper roll covers, and she gets two free tickets to get in. You can ask her yourself. Booth 43."

"Look, if you're innocent, then why don't you just let us take a look and make sure that money isn't inside your bag?" Chase's voice was even and calm.

Larry exchanged a look with his "girl." She nodded with a haughty shrug of her shoulders and rolled her eyes.

"Whatever," she muttered.

Larry pulled the bags forward and opened the paper handles on the first one. His eyes widened before we even saw what was inside.

"I have no idea how that got there." He swung his head back and forth, his eyes widening.

I peered inside. Wads of cash were spread across the bottom. If I had to guess, there was probably around a thousand dollars.

"I'm going to have to take you down to the station," Chase said, grabbing Larry's arm.

"I swear, I didn't take that money. I don't know where it came from. Someone's framing me."

Chase pulled out his handcuffs and cast a weary glance my way. "That's what they all say."

***

I could hardly wait until the bazaar ended, which was ridiculous. I was more than happy to be here. I wanted to help Greg and Babette. But I was also anxious to talk to Chase again and find out what he'd discovered about Larry Jenkins. Not even peppermint hot chocolate or peanut butter blossom cookies worked to put me in the spirit at the moment.

Ten minutes before closing, I spotted some familiar faces heading our way. Greg, Babette, and Bryan approached.

"Hey guys! It's great to see you here." I gave Greg and Babette each a gentle hug.

"Bryan convinced us that it would be good for us to get out of the house," Babette said, her face drawn with discomfort. She wore an old Christmas sweater, and Greg still sported his neck brace. "Plus, the doctor wants me to put in at least five thousand steps every day. That might sound easy for some people, but not me. Every step feels like torture."

"Maybe you found good parking spaces, at

least?" There I went, trying to look on the bright side. Maybe Cindy Lou Who had always been a secret hero of mine.

"Bryan was a dear and he dropped us off. Have I mentioned he's been good to us?" Babette leaned closer. "You're not single, are you? I'd love for him to find a nice girl."

My eyes widened. I'd always been the go-to girl for people who had strange relatives in need of a date. "Sorry, I'm taken."

"I wish he could find someone. One day." Babette glanced around. "I see that we barely got here in time, though."

"Everything closes up in a few minutes, but you still have time to look around. You can come back here before you leave and have some of our leftover goodies."

Her eyes skimmed the table. "It doesn't look like you have that much left."

"We don't. We've had good sales today." Good sales, good opportunities for theft also. I kept that part quiet.

"In case I haven't told you yet, we truly appreciate everything you're doing for us. It means a lot that you would reach out and help like this."

"It's my pleasure. I like to combat the bad in the world, one random act of kindness at a time."

"God bless you for it," Babette said. "I think I will wander around for a few minutes. I can't afford to buy anything, but it will be nice to see what's out there. Maybe it will put me in the Christmas mood. All I've felt all season is like saying, 'Bah, humbug!'"

"I hear they're giving out hot chocolate about five booths down. It might warm you up some."

As Greg and Babette wandered away, Bryan lingered behind a moment. He wore a long-sleeve polo shirt with the emblem for E.L.F. Deliveries embroidered on the lapel. I pushed the thought of Babette trying to play matchmaker to the back of my mind and instead pointed to his shirt.

"Cute name for a company."

"Thanks." He looked down at his lapel. "It works well this time of year. It's a small business right now—just six of us. But we stay busy."

Bryan's eyes met mine. "We really do appreciate all of this." He lowered his voice as he cast another glance toward the Sullivans' departing figures. "I don't think they've been completely forthcoming with you."

My shoulders tensed as I anticipated what he might say. "What do you mean?"

"Their situation is more dire than they let

on," he continued. "Greg can't work. I'm guessing Babette will end up being on disability, but it can take months for a check to come through from the government. I've been trying to buy groceries and help them out as much as I can."

"That's really kind of you."

He frowned. "Well, honestly, I feel terrible about this, like I let them down. I was supposed to go collect the money from the various locations on the very day it was stolen."

"Why didn't you?"

"I was sent to Indianapolis for a training workshop for my job. I got back too late to do anything. Anyway, I'm just telling you this because I know they would never say anything themselves. They're such a giving family. I hate to see them like this. Besides, it's the kids you worry about, you know?"

I nodded. "I do."

Maybe Bryan needed a Christmas miracle too.

Did I have any friends I could fix him up with? None that I could think of. But maybe, somehow, I could think of a special Christmas blessing for him as well.

Just then, loud voices carried from down the street. My eyes widened when I saw Dr.

Evans—the persnickety choir director from my
church—and Greg facing off.

"What in the world . . .?" I stepped toward
them.

"You stopped returning my calls," Dr. Evans
said as I approached.

"I did the job just as you asked," Greg said,
his face reddening with each word.

"It wasn't what we agreed to. My dining
room ceiling looks nothing like the picture we
looked at. Nothing."

"I explained to you that I would do my best
to match it."

"Every time I look at my ceiling, I mourn for
my money that went down the drain." Dr. Evans
narrowed his eyes.

I knew him from the worship arts team at
church, though I didn't know him well. He was only
a few years older than me, but he had a snobbish
quality about him that I'd never cared for. He was
musically talented—way talented—and apparently
he was holding out for his dream job of teaching
music at the University of Cincinnati. Until he got a
position there, he worked part-time at church and
part-time at another job. I couldn't remember what
it was at the moment, but I did recall that his
toffee-nosed attitude fit the requirements well.

"What's going on?" I asked.

Dr. Evans turned toward me, his eyes widening with recognition. "Holly. You know these people?"

"Of course, I know them. They're a lovely couple. What's the problem here?"

Dr. Evans scowled and raised his chin, obviously not happy with my assessment. "Well, I'd never encourage anyone to hire him."

With that, Dr. Evans turned on his heel and stomped away.

"That's not a problem," Greg muttered. "No one can hire me right now."

"I take it he was an unhappy customer?"

"Hard to please."

I followed his retreating form down the street. "He's hard to please as a choir member also. I'm sorry about that."

Greg shook his head. "It comes with the territory as a contractor. Don't worry about it."

Maybe I wouldn't bring up the donations that had been stolen today. Greg and Babette already had enough on their minds without me bringing up a sore subject like that. I needed to wait and find out if there was any definite news on Larry before I announced that also. No need of getting their hopes up that the culprit had been apprehended.

Too many of Greg and Babette's hopes had already been dashed, and I didn't want to add to the number.

CHAPTER 7

As my workers finished packing up, I stepped away to call Chase. With Ralph's help, I'd already secured the money in his office, reassured Tana of her innocence again, and given my undying thanks to the rest of the volunteers.

"Well? Did you put him away for life?" I asked when Chase answered.

"For life? For stealing petty cash?"

I frowned, pulling my scarf close as tiny flakes began to drop from the sky. It looked like the bazaar had ended right on time. "Okay, maybe I overstated it a bit. But what's going on?"

"The good news is that you'll get all of your money back. The bad news is that Larry is apparently innocent."

I flinched as if I'd been slapped. "That's not possible. I saw the money in his bag myself. That can't be a coincidence."

"You did see that money, but he claims he has no idea how it got in his bag. We think someone may have planted it there. His girlfriend confirmed they didn't go near your booth. It would have been a pretty brazen move. We're checking the video footage now, but I'm not expecting much to come from it. The camera angles weren't arranged for events like the Christmas bazaar."

"But . . . but—" I tried to think of a reasonable explanation, but I couldn't. Larry was such an obvious choice. However, he had looked surprised and he'd willingly let us look in his bag. Would he have done that if guilty?

"There's more. He has an alibi for the timeframe when the money was stolen from the convenience stores. The videos, of course, were time-stamped. Since the money was all stolen within a two-hour period on the same night, we didn't have to look very far to verify his alibi."

"Well, where was he?"

"He was playing Bingo. Three different people vouched for him."

"But that still doesn't explain how that money got into his bag today."

"Larry did say a man bumped into him while he was shopping. He thinks the guy could have slipped the money into the bag to implicate him."

"What? Really?"

"Well, the man was wearing a Santa hat . . .

with the Reds logo emblazoned across the front."

I paused for a moment. There was only one person I remembered being dressed like that.

It was Dr. Evans, the choir director from my church. He wouldn't . . . would he?

No, it was a coincidence. It had to be. But he did appear to have a reason to want to hurt the Sullivans. I just couldn't see him taking it this far.

I hoped I was right.

***

"You look distracted," Chase whispered in my ear, his warm breath tickling my cheek.

Around us, people mingled in a ballroom at a nearby hotel. I had joined Chase for the police department's annual holiday party. I wished I was feeling more festive, but my thoughts were preoccupied with everything going on.

"I am a little distracted." I frowned. "I'm sorry."

I stood at the edge of the room and watched as everyone else mingled in the dim lights of the ballroom. The place smelled like warm turkey, honey ham, and spicy apple pie. Christmas music played overhead—"All I Want for Christmas is You" at the moment.

I wore my cutest black dress with a festive red scarf, and Chase looked dashing in his black suit and tie. I'd run into several people I knew from my involvement in the community.

I had no reason not to enjoy the party—except for the fact that I was focusing on other people's problems.

"How much money did you raise at the bazaar?" Chase asked, still close enough for his breath to tickle my cheek.

I held my punch in my hand and occasionally took sips of the cranberry-flavored concoction. "We raised just over two thousand dollars, including the amount that was stolen and returned. Ralph donated an extra five thousand."

"So that totals seven thousand? That's fantastic."

I wanted to rejoice also, but I just couldn't bring myself to do it at the moment. "It's still a long way from saving the Sullivans' house, though."

"What about the online account?"

"We're up to $1,225. I'm hoping more will come in." I'd checked the numbers right before I came here.

"Holly, why are you beating yourself up over this?" Chase moved around to face me better. He blocked my view of the rest of the room, so I had no choice but to focus on him and this conversation.

I shrugged, not wanting to argue. It was so unbecoming—especially in social situations. "I'm not beating myself up. I just don't like it when the bad guys win."

"They're not. Something bad happened, and now you've turned the situation around. The Sullivans have more money now than they had before. Good has come from the bad."

"But, Chase, if I don't help these people, who will?"

"Certainly they have other people who can help. And I'm not saying you *shouldn't* help. I just hate to see you beating yourself up over it, especially since you've bent over backward to assist them."

"I know it might sound crazy, but God calls us to love other people. It's not enough to just preach that. We have to be God's hands and feet. In my own twisted way, that's what I'm trying to be. I would hope someone would do the same for me if the roles were reversed."

He squeezed my arm. "I know."

I sighed before taking another sip of my punch. "It still perplexes me how people can do such cruel things. I just don't understand the depravity of the human soul at times."

Chase grabbed my hand and tugged me closer. "How about we get out of here, Holly? We can go somewhere and relax. You know I'm not much into parties anyway."

"You should be here. These are your coworkers. I'll be fine."

He squinted and tilted his head uncertainly. "Are you sure?"

I nodded and handed him my drink. "I'm positive. Just let me run to the bathroom and freshen up for a moment, okay?"

"Sure thing."

I escaped across the room. I didn't want to be a killjoy, and that was how I felt tonight. I needed a moment to get myself together.

I didn't head for the closest bathroom, but instead walked to the one on the other side of the hotel lobby. There was less of a chance I'd run into someone there. I stepped inside and noted that the bathroom had a lobby of its own. It also had two couches, a fancy swirled ceiling, and rich-looking carpet that lent an uppity feel to the area.

Two sets of doors led inside the bathroom from the sitting area. I pushed through the first one I came to and was greeted on the other side with glossy black-and-green tiles, as well as the scent of bleach. It wasn't quite as fancy as the lobby, but it would work.

I was alone. That was the important thing.

I paused by the mirror a moment. The normal spark was missing from my eyes tonight. I needed to change that. Some Scrooge—or Grinch, depending on how I looked at it—wasn't going to steal my Christmas joy.

I escaped inside a stall for a moment and leaned against the door. I closed my eyes and drew in some deep breaths and lifted up a prayer.

Dear Lord, help me not forget the reason for the season. Help me remember all that I have to be thankful for. And help me figure out who stole that money.

I opened my eyes and blinked.

Darkness stretched across the bathroom. What?

I squinted and blinked again, making sure I wasn't losing my mind. Sure enough, the lights were out.

"Hello?" I blindly reached for the door handle and tried to exit the stall.

"Stay where you are, Ms. Paladin," a deep voice said in the distance. "There's something I need to tell you."

My blood went as cold as the North Pole as

I waited for what would happen next.

CHAPTER 8

I froze when I heard the voice. The last thing I wanted was to be in the dark with a strange man desiring to deliver a cryptic message. But what other choice did I have? I couldn't even see my hand in front of my face.

"Who are you?" My voice sounded shakier than I would have liked.

"I can't tell you."

I felt along the wall of the stall, wishing I had a weapon other than toilet paper. "You know there are police officers all over the place outside."

"I'm aware of that. I needed to catch you in private."

"You managed to do that. But why? Did you want to talk?"

"You need to look into the background of Greg and Babette Sullivan."

"What? Why would I do that?" Certainly I hadn't heard him correctly.

"They were involved in a scam about ten

years ago. They stole money from innocent people. I think they stole their own money from those canisters to gain sympathy."

Was this guy drunk? Another disturbing thought hit me: Had he moved closer? I hated not being able to see anything. "That's crazy."

"But is it?"

"Besides, they weren't at the bazaar yesterday until after the money had already been stolen." I hadn't meant to say it out loud, but I did.

"Are you sure about that?" The man sounded like he knew something I didn't.

"Greg and Babette didn't show up until the end. I was there."

"They ate at a Mexican restaurant around the corner. You should check it out. They had the time to grab the money, eat, and then show up later, looking innocent."

His words rushed over me. Had Greg and Babette told me they'd just arrived or had I assumed things? "Why are you doing this?"

"Because I don't want to see con artists succeed."

A *swoosh* sounded in the distance before a flash of light filled the room. The man had slipped outside and into the lobby area of the restroom, I realized. The light from outside had temporarily

CHRISTY BARRITT

filled the room.

Despite my blindness, I rushed toward the door. I pulled it open and nearly collided with someone.

A pretty black woman raised her hands and stepped back. I'd obviously scared her as much as she'd scared me.

"Sorry. The lights went out," I rushed. "Did you see someone leave here?" My hand went over my heart as I gulped in deep breaths.

A wrinkle formed between her eyebrows. "A man in a black suit. He mumbled that he worked here."

"Did you see which direction he went?"

"It looked like he was walking toward the party."

"Anything else you can remember?"

She shook her head. "I didn't see his face. But he was a white guy, average height. A black hat covered his face, though. A fedora."

"Thank you." Before I could waste any more time, I rushed from the bathroom. As I surveyed the empty hallway, my gaze came to a stop on something left on the floor.

A black fedora.

I frowned. That had been my only distinguishing clue. Whoever that man was, he would easily blend in now. Was he a cop?

I couldn't believe that. But somehow this man had sneaked into this Christmas party. He must have known who I was and followed me here, just to give me that message. That was how it appeared, at least.

I glanced around again and shook my head. The man was gone.

But I did see another familiar face. Amar Kumar, the owner of the first convenience store Chase and I visited.

What was he doing here? Was he the one who'd cornered me in the bathroom?

There was only one thing I was certain about: all I wanted for Christmas was to no longer feel so confused.

***

"The man in the bathroom was telling the truth." Chase shook his head as he stared at the computer screen in the office of my home. My mom was at a fundraiser, the Christmas tree in the background cast a soft glow about the room, and, of course, Bing sang in the background.

"I'm not even looking at police records, but there's a news article here about the Sullivans,"

Chase continued. "It's from Indiana."

"I think that's where Greg and Babette moved when they first got married." I leaned behind Chase, staring at the screen as he read aloud. "I remember Mrs. Signet talking about that."

"Greg and Babette collected donations for a family whose house supposedly burned down. However, it later turned out to be a scam. There was no family in need. The whole story was made up. Greg and Babette pocketed the cash they'd collected from the community."

"Just when you think you've heard it all . . ."

"Finally, a coworker caught on to what was happening and called the Sullivans out on their scheme," Chase continued. "He eventually went to the police, and Greg and Babette faced misdemeanor fraud. They had to serve community service hours and pay back the money."

I straightened as a weight pressed down on my chest. "I just can't believe this. Of all the things I thought might happen, the possibility of Greg and Babette deceiving us wasn't even a blip on my radar."

"This is the kind of world we live in, Holly. Like it or not."

"Not. I like it *not*." I crossed my arms, wishing I could settle my thoughts. In my quest for goodwill to all, peace on earth was eluding me. "But what does this mean for this situation? Greg and Babette didn't fake the car accident in order to gain sympathy . . . right?"

Chase swiveled in the chair to face me. "Faking a car accident would be difficult. But maybe they're twisting the facts. Maybe it's because the collision really was their fault."

"It's not beyond the realm of possibility. But I just can't see it. The money they have to pay out far exceeds what they could raise."

"Unless they faked their injuries. In the least, maybe they exaggerated them."

If Greg and Babette were con artists, fraud wasn't out of the question. I didn't want to believe someone would sink this low.

I turned the idea over in my head. "I just don't know, Chase. I don't want to believe they'd do this. I saw their eyes—they looked hurting."

"I'm not saying they're not hurting." His voice sounded gentle and calm. "People that desperate have a lot of things going on inside that we can't see with the human eye. What you want to believe and reality aren't always the same thing, unfortunately."

"I know . . . but this just seems extreme. Besides, wouldn't the Sullivans want all the money they could get? You'd think they'd want me to go to the media so they could bring in more cash if that was their end goal."

Chase raised a finger in thought. "Unless they're afraid someone would discover what they're doing if you went public with it."

I closed my eyes. Was that it? Was that the real reason why I couldn't do a press campaign to help the Sullivans raise money?

And, if all of this was true, then I'd just raised money for con artists.

"There's one other thing that bugs me. The light switch at the hotel: it's operated by a key. Who would have access to that?" I'd gone back to check it out before I left.

"Maybe someone swiped the key."

I nibbled on my bottom lip a moment. "Maybe. It just seems extreme for someone to do that, just so they could cast suspicions on Greg and Babette. I did see Amar."

"He took some of the management from his three stores out for a Christmas dinner. He has an alibi," Chase reminded me.

We'd tracked him down before leaving the hotel and asked him some unassuming questions. He hadn't acted guilty. Besides—what in the world could his motive possibly be? Was he in financial trouble? It just didn't make sense. Furthermore, he wasn't the man from the photos. I supposed he could have hired someone to steal the canisters for him, but that seemed extreme for such a small payout.

Chase pulled me down into his lap and wrapped his arms around my waist. "Maybe we could just forget about this for a while. I was looking forward to enjoying the holidays with you. Something uncomplicated. You know, I haven't had very many idyllic Christmases. I haven't had any, truth be told."

That had been my original goal, back before I got sidetracked with all of this. I'd wanted Chase to have a Christmas to remember. I'd practically ruined his Christmas party, and now I was obsessed with a thief. Maybe Chase was the real loser in all of this. I couldn't let that happen.

I draped my arms around his neck. "I know. And I'm looking forward to you being with my family during this season. How about this? Let's go watch a Christmas movie. I promise to let this go— for the rest of the day, at least."

"If that's the best I can get, then I'll take it."

As I stared up into his blue eyes, I realized I had to get focused. I'd be perfectly content to stay here feeling safe and wrapped in his arms. But I couldn't let the Christmas music, the soft lights, and the man of my dreams play on my sensibilities. *"White Christmas*?"

"I've heard so much about this movie."

I stood and grabbed his hand, tugging him toward the living room. "But you've never seen it. That's a shame. Everyone needs to watch it."

"You practically took the words right out of my mouth." His eyes twinkled.

"Let's remedy this. I even have some leftover cookies. It's going to be a great Christmas. At least, if I have anything to do with it."

CHAPTER 9

As soon as church was over the next morning, I decided I needed to confront the issue of Greg and Babette's past head-on. Before I arranged for the Christmas tree to be delivered and recruited little elves to help decorate at the Sullivan's house, I needed answers. I hated to be taken advantage of, and that's exactly how I was feeling.

Chase insisted on accompanying me to their house, and I didn't refuse. But I noticed the Sullivans' place seemed especially quiet as we approached the front door. I rang the bell but heard nothing. I rang the bell again. Still nothing. No scampering footsteps, blaring TV, or muted conversations.

"I don't think they're here," Chase said. "Maybe they're at church?"

"Maybe." I sighed and glanced around like the answers to all my questions might magically appear. "I'd call them, but I need to look them in the eye when I ask the questions. Besides, they no longer have phone service."

"What now?"

"There's only one other way I can think to find answers about the validity of the accident. We can ask Larry Jenkins."

Chase twisted his head, looking skeptical. "I'm not sure that's a good idea. Larry isn't the nicest man. I'm not sure he'd be forthcoming with answers."

"No, but we could get a feel for the accident. Don't you think? Isn't that what this boils down to? Did the accident happen as they claimed or not? If it really happened, then maybe the Sullivans truly do need the money. But I refuse to participate in something dishonest. I won't raise money for a family who is trying to con people."

"I suppose it's worth a shot."

Just as we reached Chase's Jeep, a car pulled to a stop on the street.

It was Bryan. I wondered how much he knew about his cousin's scam? Should I ask him, or would I just be inserting him into the middle of an ugly situation if I did? I didn't want to increase family tensions.

I chewed on the thought a moment.

He spotted me and called out, "You looking for Greg and Babette?"

"Yes, as a matter of fact, I am."

"They're at a luncheon after church. Anything I can help you with?"

I shrugged, wanting to keep my mouth shut. Yet my hunger for answers also pulled at me. "I wanted to check and see how they're feeling."

Bryan shrugged. "They have good days and bad days, I suppose. Sometimes they seem fine, and other times the aches and pains come back."

Could that be because they were faking it all?

I shifted. "Bryan, how long have you lived with them?"

"For a few years."

"So you didn't live with them when they were out in Indiana?"

He shook his head. "I was in college down in Kentucky then. Why do you ask?"

"Just wondering." I smiled, hoping to put him at ease. "That's nice of you to help your cousin like this."

He shrugged, like it was no big deal. "Family looks out for each other, right? They stuck with me when times were rough, so now I'll stick with them." He shifted. "By the way, any news on the money that was stolen?"

I shook my head. "No, not yet. I'm sorry."

"Hopefully you'll know something soon. It seems like donations aren't safe anywhere anymore, are they? Whoever the thief is, he's brazen to steal from both the convenience store and bazaar."

"Yes, he is."

Bryan shifted and glanced at his watch. "In the meantime, do you want me to tell Greg and Babette you stopped by?"

"No, that's okay. I'll catch them again later." And I'd catch them by surprise, I figured. The less warning they had, the better.

***

Twenty minutes later, Chase and I pulled up to a skinny, rundown house on the north side of town. A late-model Oldsmobile sat in the driveway with the front bumper smashed like an accordion.

"It appears there really was an accident," I told Chase. "I'm surprised he still has the car."

Chase squatted to examine the vehicle. "He could have requested to get it back from impound. It can be a complicated process. The insurance company will give it back, even when totaled, but you usually don't get as much money for it."

"I'd like to talk to Larry anyway." Before

Chase could stop me, I charged up to the front door and knocked. Larry answered a moment later, wearing a wife beater T-shirt and with a toothpick dangling from his mouth. His eyes narrowed when he recognized me.

"What are you doing here, Cindy Lou Who?" he growled. "You want to accuse me of something again?"

Well, yeah, I kind of did. For stealing Christmas or at least attempting to.

Some of the anger on his face disappeared when he saw Chase. Probably not because he liked Chase but because he remembered Chase was a cop and could arrest him if things turned ugly.

"I have a question about your accident," I started.

"What about it?"

"I'd like to hear your version of what happened that day."

He crossed his arms and leaned against the doorframe of his grape juice purple house. "My version? What are you talking about, *my* version?"

"You said the accident was Greg and Babette's fault."

"That's right. They ran that red light, causing me to T-bone them. Look at my car. It tells the story better than I do."

I couldn't deny that his car was a mangled mess. "Did they seem injured afterward?"

"Beats me." He spit and then put the toothpick back into his mouth. "I had to be carried away on a stretcher. I wasn't really paying attention to anyone else at that point in time."

"You seem okay now," I pointed out. "Are you?"

"Thank goodness—yes. I am good. But I was sore for about a month. It could have been worse. There were two witnesses at the scene who saw them run that light. Why else would I even be allowed to bring them to court otherwise?"

That was a good question.

"Do you have the names of these witnesses?" I asked. Chase would probably be able to get them from the police reports, but I thought asking Larry might save some time.

"As a matter of fact, I do. I had to get them for insurance purposes." Larry pulled out his phone and hit a few buttons. A moment later, he spouted out two names and addresses. I quickly typed them into my phone.

After we said goodbye and as we walked to Chase's Jeep, his phone beeped. "It's work. I've got to go in, Holly. There's a new lead on one of my cases."

I nodded. "I understand. I have Christmas choir practice in a little while anyway."

"I'll drop you off at your house then, and we'll reconnect later. Sound good?"

I was just about to say, "Sounds great" when Chase muttered, "Cindy Lou Who."

His eyes sparkled with so much amusement that I couldn't help but punch him in the arm.

I was never going to live that nickname down.

***

As soon as Chase dropped me off, I called Jamie. She picked me up a few minutes later in her beat-up minivan, better known as the Ghettomobile. Jamie had named it that, not me. I quickly updated her on what was going on.

"All of that has transpired since we talked last?" she asked. "You know what transpired in my life during that time? I got my little brothers ready for bed, I slept, and I went to church."

"It's crazy, isn't it? I suppose it proves that persistence can pay off. On the other hand, though, I want to spread Christmas cheer and kindness, and I know there are people out there who truly need help, I don't want to waste my time with fakers."

"I agree. I hope Greg and Babette wouldn't do something this deplorable." She glanced at me as we cruised down the road. "I'm assuming you wanted me to drive because of the van?"

She'd caught me. "It's the only bad thing about my Mustang. It's recognizable."

"I'm always happy to be of service. Just tell me where to go."

Ten minutes later, we pulled across the street from the Sullivans' house. I didn't even start to get out. Instead, I settled back into my seat and watched.

"What are you doing?"

"I want to see if Greg or Babette come out."

"Why?"

"Because they're probably not going to own up to faking their injuries. But I could catch them walking like they're just fine or without a neck brace."

She nodded. "I tell you what, if you decide to switch careers, you should be a P.I. Insurance companies hire people for stuff like this."

"So I've heard. I really don't want to make a habit of doing surveillance. Why is it that I always start with good intentions but end up being embroiled in messes?" I sighed and looked down at my candy-cane painted fingernails.

"It's easy to stay out of messes when you're sitting on the sidelines. Once you get into the fight, it's never pretty."

"It's true. But I'd rather live life in the thick of things than as a mere observer." I took a sip of my coffee. "However, sitting here for hours feels very much like observing."

"You said Larry verified that accident was real, right?"

I nodded. "Yeah, but something still doesn't feel quite right. Someone isn't telling the whole truth."

"And you think this all connects back with the missing money?"

"I'm not sure how it all fits. But it does. Somehow. I'm going to figure out how."

"The thing I don't get is this: why would the Sullivans steal their own money?" Jamie asked. "That doesn't make sense."

"I agree. I don't know, Jamie. But something's not right, and I'm determined to find some answers. I even wonder if Dr. Evans has something to do with this."

"Dr. Evans?"

"The choir director from my church."

Her eyebrows shot up. "Oh, him. I've never cared for him."

"Me neither. He has a reason not to like the Sullivans. Apparently Greg did some supposedly shoddy plasterwork for him. He was also wearing a Reds Santa hat at the bazaar. But he seems like the type who'd use a more clever way of getting revenge, not the type to steal canisters."

"People will surprise you, though."

"I can't deny that."

Silence stretched for a few minutes.

"Don't you need to go Christmas shopping or something? I mean, it's a busy time of year, and you're getting mixed up in the middle of all of this?"

I shrugged. "I started making things for people back in August. Scarves for the men. Jewelry for my mom and sister. I baked some orange-cranberry bread and froze it to give to the neighbors. I have a few other things up my sleeve. Like, I found this great charity where I can give monetary gifts in people's names. I mean, really . . . we all have so much. Why feed the materialism?"

"Stuff doesn't make you happy. That's for sure."

"Some people will never realize that. It's a shame." I elbowed Jamie. "Look, there's Babette."

She walked from the house, a bag of trash in her hands. Sure enough, she was still limping.

But, if I remembered correctly, didn't she have a bad knee? It seemed like somewhere in the recesses of my mind, I remembered something about a knee replacement surgery she'd had several years ago. Mrs. Signet had a tendency to overshare and talk . . . a lot.

"She's definitely limping," Jamie said, slumping low in her seat.

I made a quick decision. "I'm not going to confront them. Not yet."

"What do you want to do instead?"

"I'm going to go talk to a couple of witnesses from the accident. I just want to corroborate their stories. Because if I'm wrong then I've just sabotaged everything I stand for . . . and that would make me a Scrooge."

Jamie gasped, echoing the horror I felt at the mere suggestion.

There was no way Holly Anna Paladin was going to rain on someone else's Christmas parade.

CHAPTER 10

A quick Internet search helped me find the first
witness whose name Larry Jenkins had given me:
Allison Daniels. We pulled up in front of her
ramshackle house, and I stared at it a moment. A
huge blow-up reindeer stood in the front yard, but
he was lopsided and almost looked in pain. A
strand of Christmas lights stretched across the roof,
but part of them hung down low, like a clip had
fallen off, and the other half looked like they were
being tugged toward the ground by the outlet
where they were plugged in.

"So, you have a story concocted, or are you
just going with the truth?" Jamie asked.

I nibbled on my bottom lip for a moment.
"I'm not completely sure. It would be nice in times
like this to have an official title, wouldn't it? Saying
I'm simply a concerned citizen who wants to ask
really nosy questions doesn't fly."

"We can always use my job title as a cover
story. Reporters are always looking for

information."

I nodded. "Maybe that would be the best idea."

We'd used it several times in the past, and it had been quite effective.

Before I could exit the van, the front door to the house opened. I watched carefully as two women paused to talk inside, their backs toward me. One had dark hair, and the other was more of a redhead.

Otherwise, it was hard to tell much about them. I supposed this would be a good time to go introduce myself, but something internal urged me to wait.

"A Marshmallow World" blared over the radio, the happy song a sharp contrast to the tension I felt in my gut.

"You okay?" Jamie asked.

I stared harder, waiting for whatever realization that lurked below the surface to rush to the top.

As soon as the women stepped outside, I knew what was wrong.

That was Larry Jenkins' girlfriend talking to Allison Daniels!

She was a friend with one of the witnesses.

I bit down. I knew what this meant.

It meant that, as usual, things weren't as they seemed.

**

I couldn't concentrate during the final choir practice before our performance tomorrow night. I was participating in a citywide choir, which was taking place at the megachurch where I'd grown up. The choir probably had fifty members from all over town, and the whole experience had been fun.

I kept my little black binder with sheet music in front of me. I sang alto, and we were in the middle of "Joy to the World" in the massive sanctuary of my church when I saw Chase step through the back door and cross his arms. I'd texted him earlier and told him we needed to talk ASAP.

I licked my lips and made a quick choice. With apology in my voice, I slipped across the risers, trying my best not to step on shiny black loafers or expensive high heels. I heard several "umps" and "ohs" and other sounds of irritated exclamation. The space was tight, and people could barely see me over their choir binders until I'd already bumped into them.

Dr. Evans gave me a teacherly look of scorn from over the top of his half-frame glasses. He treated us like we were part of Mannheim Steamroller and getting paid big bucks. He ran a tight ship, even though the choir members were volunteers.

When I finally finished disrupting practice, I scampered down the steps leading to the massive stage and practically skipped to Chase.

"That was a sight to behold." His voice lilted with amusement.

I took his arm and led him into the foyer so I wouldn't interrupt the rehearsal any more than I already had. As strains about heaven and nature singing rolled in the background, I shut the heavy wooden door to the sanctuary.

"Thanks for coming," I murmured.

"It sounded important. What's going on?"

As I told him what Jamie and I had discovered, his face twisted with different emotions. Surprise. Aggravation. Realization.

"It must have been a staged auto accident," he muttered, shaking his head and staring off into the distance.

"What's that?"

"It's just what it sounds like. People are doing it more and more often. They carefully plan for accidents to happen in order to collect the insurance money. This may not have been the Sullivans' fault. It could have been Larry Jenkins."

I let his words sink in. "So he T-boned the Sullivans on purpose?"

Chase nodded. "These people who do this are truly amazing. They'll signal for someone to pull over in traffic and, when the other driver does, they'll merge also and collide with them. Afterward, of course, they'll claim no responsibility and deny that they ever motioned for the person to move over."

"And, let me guess, they find witnesses who are actually people they know?" I remembered seeing Larry's girlfriend with Allison Daniels.

"Bingo. They make sure they have one or two friends around—friends who claim they don't know each other. They'll act as witnesses and tell the police that the other driver didn't signal or that the light was red or whatever they need to say to get away with it. That's how the accidents happen. I'd say there was a good chance Greg really didn't run that red light. He was, however, in the wrong place at the wrong time."

"I heard Larry had another auto accident earlier this year."

"We're looking into that one also."

The more I learned, the more unsettled I felt. "What can we do, Chase?"

"We?" His eyebrows shot up. "Nothing. I'll take it from here, Holly."

"But—"

"You have enough on your plate. You worry about the Sullivans. Speaking of which, did you ever talk to them about the Indiana incident?"

I shook my head. "That's what I plan to do next."

"If they're innocent in all of this, then you're running out of time to ensure they have a merry Christmas. I know you don't want that."

I nodded like a sailor might when he received his orders. "You're right. I'm focusing on the Sullivans."

He grinned and kissed the tip of my nose. "You're cute, Holly."

"I've got to get to work."

"Go get 'em, Cindy Lou Who."

CHAPTER 11

After choir practice, I decided to stop by the Sullivans again. I had to talk to them and find out the truth. But before I got down to the nitty-gritty, half of the church choir volunteered to join me. Part of them sang Christmas carols outside the front door, while the rest barged into the Sullivans' house with a Christmas tree.

As we finished "O Come All Ye Faithful," Dr. Evans stepped forward. "I'd like to apologize for my tirade on Saturday. It wasn't very Christlike of me, and I've felt poorly about myself ever since then."

My heart lifted at Dr. Evans' words. I hated to see believers not getting along. To show love and compassion went so much farther than showing bitterness and holding grudges.

"We appreciate the apology," Greg said from his perch in the doorway.

"I hope we at least spread some Christmas joy."

"You did. Thank you."

Babette and Greg looked grateful but somber. Why was that?

As soon as the choir left, I asked Babette if I could come inside for a moment.

"Of course," she said, pushing the door open. "Thank you for the tree and for trying to spread some Christmas cheer."

When I stepped inside, it was a madhouse. All the kids were home, as well as Mrs. Signet and Bryan. Boxes were scattered everywhere. The older kids and Bryan were acting like typical brothers and sisters. Bryan yelled something about dirty socks, and the oldest boy yelled back that Bryan liked to wear "griddles." The two tackled each other.

"What's going on?" I asked.

"We got notice that we had to be out. The bank is taking our house."

My lower jaw dropped open. "What? At Christmastime?"

Babette nodded, wiping away the tears from her eyes. "It's true. I wish it weren't. Apparently the notice came in the mail on Friday, but we didn't open the letter until today. You get tired of seeing all of the bills."

"I can imagine."

"Holly Anna!" someone said, walking toward me with outstretched arms. Mrs. Signet. Of course. Guilt pounded in my heart.

"Hi, Mrs. Signet." I returned her hug.

"I'm so glad you're here. You're such a blessing throughout this nastiness, as is Bryan. Thank you for your help."

Guilt pounded harder. "You're welcome." I cleared my throat and turned to Babette. "Actually, I was wondering if I could speak to you and Greg for a moment."

A new emotion rushed through Babette's eyes. Was it fear? Concern? Maybe just curiosity. I wasn't sure.

Babette called Greg, and the three of us stepped out onto the porch. Greg still wore his neck brace and Babette limped.

"First, let me start by saying that I believe Larry Jenkins staged the car accident with you."

"What?"

I nodded. "Apparently, it's the hot new thing. People devise ways to have fender benders, make it look like it was the other driver's fault, and then they collect the insurance money."

"I knew there was something off about that man," Greg muttered.

I shifted, feeling uncomfortable at the next subject. I couldn't avoid it, though. "There's one other thing I need to tell you. I know about what happened in Indiana. I know about the fake account you set up for an imaginary family whose house burned down."

Babette glanced at Greg before wobbling her head back and forth slowly. "I was afraid that might come out."

"What happened? Is it true?"

Babette looked at Greg once more before nodding. "I wish it weren't true. But it was."

"We were going through a hard time," Greg chimed in. He lowered himself into a rusty metal chair and let out a long sigh. "I knew if people found out about that then no one would want to help us. Maybe we deserve it."

I leaned against the porch railing and crossed my arms, my wool coat barely keeping me warm. A cold front had swept through, and the wind felt wicked. "What would lead you to do something like that? Please, help me to understand."

"Have you ever known what it was like to not have enough money for groceries?" Babette asked.

My heart pounded in my chest. "I have to say no, I've never been there before."

"That's the point we were at. They cut back Greg's hours at work—this was before he owned his own business. I was at home on bed rest with my pregnancy. I also had two little ones running around, and I had no one to help me with them. If we moved back home to Mom's house, then Greg would have to drive an hour-and-a-half to his job. It seemed like a no-win situation."

"So you scammed people out of money?"

Babette squeezed the skin between her eyes. "We didn't mean it like that. But we saw so many other friends who were prosperous. They didn't know what it was like to want for anything. And here we were, struggling financially. Again. We made all the right choices, but we were still being punished, it seemed. We didn't know what else to do. I couldn't exactly go back to work. Greg looked for a second job, but he couldn't find anything."

"I know times can be tight sometimes," I finally said, compassion and justice colliding inside me. I still wasn't sure which one would win.

"A friend out in California had their house burn down. Through a community fundraiser, they were able to collect around ten thousand dollars for the family. We knew it was wrong. We knew we shouldn't do it. But when you're at wit's end, you'll do things you never imagined you could do."

"Is that what you're doing now?" I asked quietly.

"No! Of course not." Babette's wide eyes latched onto mine. "What you don't know is that when we got on our feet again, we paid that money back. I felt so terrible during that time. I vowed I would never do it again. Never."

I didn't say anything.

"You don't believe me, do you?" Babette asked.

"I didn't say that."

"Here. Look at this. It's proof about our situation now." She thrust a paper in my hands.

It was her foreclosure notice. And it looked real.

After a moment, I nodded. "I believe you. But this puts me back to square one. I have no idea who's behind the thefts, but I'm going to keep trying to raise that money to help you."

***

That evening, Chase was back at work and Jamie was babysitting her siblings so her parents could Christmas shop.

I sat in my home office, trying to get into the Christmas spirit, but I couldn't stop thinking about the Sullivans. Was I really back to the start? That didn't seem possible.

I made a list of what I knew so far.

The man who'd stolen the canisters was relatively young—probably in his late twenties or early thirties.

He was white, average height, average build.

He liked the Cincinnati Reds.

He probably lived in the Price Hill area, based on the stores where the canisters had been stolen.

He seemed to have a personal vendetta against Greg and Babette.

He'd most likely been at the Christmas bazaar and somehow escaped undetected.

He was aware of the incident with Larry Jenkins. He had to be because he'd planted the money in Larry's bags.

He somehow had access to the key to the hotel restrooms because he'd turned the lights off.

The culprit had also somehow known I was going to be at the party at the hotel.

Put all of that together, and who did you have?

That was the question of the hour.

Identifying the man simply from his photo on the security video seemed unlikely, like finding Waldo in a sea of Santas.

Spontaneously, I picked up the phone and called a friend from church who worked at a local hotel and asked her which employees generally had access to bathroom keys. The list seemed long and included management, the front desk, and janitors.

Did any of my suspects have connections with the hotel? Did anyone know my schedule as well as the Sullivans' schedule? Who had motive, means, and opportunity?

I chewed on the questions a few more minutes.

The plasterwork at the hotel was amazing . . . could Greg have done it? If so, did that mean he had access to the hotel bathrooms? But that wouldn't make any sense because why would he implicate himself by delivering that cryptic message to me there?

Amar Kumar was at the hotel that day, celebrating with his management team. Could he have swiped the key from someone? He still didn't have a motive, though, and as hard I tried to find one, I couldn't.

Dr. Evans had apologized, but was that just a distraction? Would he have gone so far as to steal money from the Sullivans? I didn't want to believe it. He had been at the bazaar, though. If I remembered correctly, he worked part-time as a concierge somewhere. Maybe at the hotel where Chase's police party had been?

The idea of Bryan being guilty had briefly fluttered through my mind. But he'd said he was at a training session in Indy when the thefts occurred. Besides, he seemed to honestly love his family and want to help.

Then there was Larry Jenkins. Was he somehow still connected? I'd pretty much ruled him out, but maybe that was a mistake.

I sighed. What if there was another suspect I was missing entirely? Some sort of small detail kept nagging at the back of my mind. Something that I must have missed. But what was it?

The answer smacked me in the face.

Could it be? How could I have missed that detail?

I leaned back and tapped on my chin a moment. I had an idea, but I needed to make a few calls to confirm my theory.

I might be able to even catch the thief, if my idea panned out.

But I was going to need some help. I had to get busier than Santa's elves on the night before Christmas if I was going to make this work.

CHAPTER 12

Nervous flutters swarmed wildly in my stomach as I held the choir binder in front of me in preparation for tonight's concert.

This was going to work, I told myself. It had to. Otherwise, Jamie was right, and *I* was the one who'd end up being a Scrooge.

Dr. Evans walked backstage and barked, "Is everyone ready?"

The choir members mumbled, "Yes," and we lined up and headed out front. My shoulders felt tense as I took my place on the risers and gazed out at everyone filling the pews. The church probably held seven hundred people, and there didn't appear to be an empty seat in the house.

My gaze scanned the crowds. Near the front, I spotted my family—my mom and Ralph, as well as my sister, Alex, and her husband, William. Chase sat beside them, giving me a little wink. He knew what was going on. I'd gotten his stamp of approval before proceeding, which was a step in the right direction for me.

Jamie was also here with her family, as well as several people from the youth center. The rest of the faces blended together. It was hard to tell one from the other. People from all around town liked to come for the church's annual Christmas cantata. It was a great way to be reminded about the real reason for the season.

Most importantly, I spotted Mrs. Signet, Greg, Babette, Bryan, and all of the children. Perfect. I'd invited them last night and told them it was imperative that they come. They didn't realize yet that they were the guests of honor.

Pastor Stephens had agreed that we could collect a love offering for the family. I considered this a win-win. The family would get money, and the whole process would allow me to catch the person behind these thefts.

I hoped.

After the pastor said a few words to the audience, Dr. Evans turned to us, tapped his baton on the music stand, and we all stood at attention. The music began playing from the mini-orchestra located in a makeshift pit below the stage. We sang "Carol of the Bells," but I was having trouble concentrating.

Jesus. Focus on Jesus.

While some people got distracted by commercialism, I got distracted by philanthropy. I suppose both could be negative, at least if they took my focus off of the gratefulness I should feel when I considered the fact that the Savior of the world came to earth as a baby, and later died for my sins before rising again.

I had to bring the sacrifice of praise to Him at this moment, and that meant giving my attention to earnest worship. Not showmanship. Not bringing glory to myself. Not making an idol out of helping other people.

Right now I had to focus on Jesus.

The rest of the cantata passed with ease. The music absorbed me as the words of the songs flowed like a prayer from my heart.

I was thankful for Christmas. Thankful for the real meaning of the season. Sure, I loved the other Christmas traditions that came with this time of year. I liked decorating and baking and presents and lights.

But, mostly, I liked celebrating Jesus.

As the concert ended, the flutters in my stomach returned. This was where our plan would be set into motion.

Dr. Evans turned to the crowd. "We have a

family here tonight who has gone through the tragic circumstances of a car accident that has left them with health problems. As these things go, bills have been piling up. Tonight, we're asking the community to step up and help to spread some Christmas cheer. If you feel inclined, we're asking you to give a donation to the family. The offering plates will be passed."

My hands were sweaty now. So much could go wrong. But so much could also go right. If the thief was here, he would be salivating right now.

Chase stood. He was going to help take up the collection, which would also allow him to keep an eye on the money.

I felt certain the person behind these thefts was here tonight. I also felt certain he would strike again. The amount collected this evening would probably be bigger than any of the previous ones. And this would be the perfect opportunity to hit the Sullivans where it hurt.

A few minutes later, the choir was dismissed from the stage and everyone was invited to a church social out in the fellowship hall. Meanwhile, the money would be counted in the finance office, and the door would be left unlocked.

If everything went according to plan, the

culprit would sneak into the office and try to steal the money. Chase and I would catch him red-handed, and this headache would be over faster than I could list the Twelve Days of Christmas.

Chase and I stood against the wall in the fellowship hall. Across the room, people surrounded the Sullivans, offering them encouragement and warm smiles. It was a beautiful sight.

"You did great," Chase said.

I straightened the tailored jacket of my red dress. "All of this could backfire. I could be wrong."

"If the MO of this guy is correct, he's here tonight, somewhere among these faces. He won't be able to resist making a move. When he does, we'll catch him."

Pastor Stephens approached us with a wide grin. "I just checked with the treasurer. So far we've collected almost ten thousand dollars for the Sullivans."

"That's wonderful," I murmured.

"All but fifty dollars will be locked in the safe," he continued. "Everything is on schedule for our guys to leave the office at 9:30 sharp."

"We'll take it from there," Chase said.

"I hope this works," the pastor continued. "It's not the way we normally do things around here."

"The police department thanks you for your cooperation," Chase said.

Other officers were waiting in the parking lot in case things went wrong. I truly hoped nothing would.

I glanced at my watch. "We have about five minutes."

Chase nodded across the distance. "There's a surprising face. It's Amar Kumar."

Amar approached us and offered a quick, curt nod. "Detective. Miss."

"Fancy seeing you here," I told him, my gaze still surveying the rest of the crowd. I thought I knew exactly who the thief was. I had a clear image in my mind of whom I was drawing out. But what if I was wrong?

"My wife, Veena, sings with the choir."

My eyes widened as I pictured the lovely, soft-spoken woman I'd briefly gotten to know. "Veena is your wife? She sings a lovely soprano."

Amar nodded. "That she does. I thought you looked familiar when you came into my store. I must have seen you when I picked her up from practice before."

That had been why he'd given me that look on the day we'd first met. "Of course."

"It's great to see you, Amar," I said, afraid time would get away from us. "If you'll excuse us a moment, though."

"Of course."

Chase and I slipped from the social and walked toward the finance office. Instead of going inside the room, we disappeared into the library across the hall and kept the lights off.

"Here goes nothing," I muttered. "The carrot is dangling. Now we have to see if the culprit takes the bait."

We waited in the darkness, eyes pressed close to the crack in the door. Nothing happened.

The happy sounds from the church social drifted down the hallway to the quiet solitude of the administrative area.

Finally, I saw a shadow moving in front of the door.

"It worked! Someone's trying to get in the office!" I whispered.

We waited a few minutes until the door across the hall closed. Then Chase and I made our move.

We crept from the library and moved to either side of the office door. At Chase's signal, we burst into the room and flipped on the lights.

Sure enough, Bryan Sullivan stood at the

desk, his hand buried in the offering plate.

He raised his hands when he saw us and dropped the dollar bills. "Wow. I wasn't expecting this. I was just . . . checking on the money. Greg asked me to."

I shook my head, anger heating my cheeks. "Tell the truth, Bryan. You're behind the thefts."

Sweat sprinkled across his upper lip and his gaze skittered all over the room, almost as if he was looking for an easy escape. "I don't know what you're talking about."

I stepped closer, raising my chin higher to let him know I wouldn't be making this easy on him. "Admit it, Bryan. You're the guilty party here. You weren't out of town with E.L.F. Deliveries when that money was stolen. In fact, you were making runs that day—in the same area where the convenience stores were located. Of course, your truck was too big and obvious to park in the lots, so you had to park on the side streets, which really worked in your favor."

"I don't know what you're talking about." He wiped his forehead and shifted uncomfortably. His gaze jerked behind us again, as if he hadn't given up on making a run for it.

"You're the same size, height, build, and age as the suspect," I continued. "Apparently, you really do wear a 'griddle,' and that's why you looked thinner in the videos."

He scoffed before stepping back a nudge and raising his hands in a silent "back off" motion. "Those are all just guesses or coincidences."

"I confirmed that Greg did some work at the Mulligan Hotel downtown before his accident," I said, pacing slightly as I formed my thoughts. "You found a key he used there, and you used it at the party that night to cast suspicion on your cousin."

"Holly, you've got this all wrong. I would never do that. I was trying to help. Just like you. We're both good people, cut from the same cloth."

"Oh no. Don't even go there." I shook my head, repulsed that some people could be this selfish. "You mentioned the money that had been stolen from the bazaar when I never mentioned it to you or your cousin. I should have realized your slip up right away, but I had too much on my mind."

His eyes widened and he swallowed hard. "Of course, you mentioned it. How else would I have known?"

"I almost missed it myself, but I made it a point not to tell Greg or Babette because I didn't want to add any more stress for them," I continued. "You went to the Mexican restaurant with your cousin and Babette that day. Only, after you dropped them off, you swung by the bazaar and stole the money."

"Don't be ridiculous."

I wasn't going to stop now. I was on a roll. "You tried to pin the theft on Larry Jenkins, figuring he was the perfect culprit. You obviously did some research on the man since you recognized him. Then at the bazaar, the opportunity to frame him was practically handed to you. And you were right—Larry *was* the perfect culprit. But this is one crime he was innocent of. You should be ashamed of yourself."

I almost added "young man," but I stopped myself. We *were* about the same age, after all. It was too early in my life to have my mother emerge from me.

"I know this looks bad, but I'm innocent." He wasn't giving up, was he? Maybe he figured if he denied it long enough, then we would have nothing to hold him on. He had no idea how persistent I could be.

I frowned and paused from my pacing for long enough to tap my chin. "The only thing I can't figure out is why you would do this. Why you would sell out your own family."

A gasp sounded behind us, and I turned in

time to see Greg and Babette standing in the doorway.

"Bryan?" Babette gasped. "It was you this whole time?"

"I don't know what they're talking about." His voice changed from defensive to whiny and victim-like.

"We're family, Bryan," Greg said. "We trusted you. We let you into our home."

Bryan's frown deepened. "I would never let down family. We're there for each other."

"I thought the leather jacket the man wore in the security video looked like yours," Babette said, her hand still over her mouth as if to stop it from gaping open in horror. "I just didn't want to believe it."

At that moment, Bryan must have known he was caught because his face transformed from insistent victim to hostile culprit.

"I don't know why you look so outraged," he said, bitterness creeping into his voice. "The two of you are the ones who are experts at conning people, right? You stole money from other people and got away with it. You stole money from me and from half of the community. And what did you get? A slap on the wrist."

Babette's mouth opened wider. "You know

we feel terrible about that. It was a terrible lapse in judgment, but we've paid for that crime . . . so you're saying you *are* behind this?"

Bryan scowled and shook his head. "I don't know what to say."

"Why? Would you at least tell us why?" Greg said. "We deserve that much, don't we? Is it revenge for our past mistakes?"

Bryan sighed. "It's not just that. Now I'm supporting you. I know you depend on my contribution for the house payment every month. Since all of this happened, I can't move out. I figured if you lost your home you'd move in with Babette's mom, and then I'd be free."

"We could have just talked about these things." Greg's shoulders slumped. "You didn't have to take it this far."

Bryan crossed his arms. "People should pay for their mistakes."

"We did," Babette said. "I'm sorry you don't see that."

"Justice wasn't served."

"Bryan, we're sorry," Greg said. "We truly are."

"It's more than that," Bryan continued. "I keep trying to move out, but then I'm guilted into staying. I couldn't leave you all, knowing you had all of these bills piling up. But I couldn't stay either. I was never going to get away and never going to get ahead in my life if I kept living with you."

"All you had to do was tell us." Greg rubbed his temples as hurt and betrayal stained his gaze. "We would have understood."

"Would you have? You would have told me it was okay, but I knew how much hurt it would cause."

"Do you realize how much hurt *this* has caused?" Babette asked quietly.

"I never expected all this to happen." Bryan sneered at me. "She was never supposed to get involved."

"Thank goodness Holly did," Babette said. "You might have gotten away with this otherwise."

An officer appeared at the door and cuffed Bryan. He hauled him into the hallway and left us all standing in the office looking at each other for a moment.

"Do you want to press charges?" Chase asked.

Babette and Greg exchanged a look, and finally Greg shook his head. "I don't know. After all the kindness and forgiveness shown to us, it seems unfair to press charges against Bryan. Besides, it's not in the spirit of Christmas."

"The difference is that when people showed you kindness and forgiveness you also showed a repentant spirit. That seems to be lacking in Bryan," I said softly.

"I agree," Chase said. "He doesn't see anything wrong with what he did. Maybe facing some repercussions for his crime will help him see the light."

I stepped closer to Chase. "Don't lose hope. If Scrooge can change—and the Grinch too, for that matter—then so can Bryan. Don't give up on him."

"We won't." A small smile lit Babette's face. "And there is good news. We just heard from the pastor about how much money was raised. It's enough to catch us up on house payments. He also introduced us to a financial counselor who thinks she can help us reduce some of our bills. I think everything is going to work out."

"It will, Babette. I have faith." I smiled, grateful that everything seemed to be working out. Maybe the Sullivans really would have a merry Christmas this year.

CHAPTER 13

Christmas morning dawned bright and early. I felt like a child as I hopped out of bed before six a.m. and made myself decent. I still wore my adorable snowflake pajamas, but I brushed my teeth, added a touch of makeup, and made sure my hair was pulled into a neat ponytail. Then I rushed downstairs, started some coffee, and stuck the coffeecake into the oven so it would be nice and warm by the time people arrived.

Right on time, the doorbell rang at seven. My family flooded inside, along with Chase.

"Merry Christmas," Chase told me, pecking my lips with a quick kiss.

His arms were loaded with gifts. I smiled when I saw the way the presents were wrapped. The edges weren't even or neatly tucked, but making things beautiful wasn't Chase's area of expertise. The wrapping fit Chase, though, and I was grateful he was here with us.

A few months ago, I'd wondered if I might

get a ring for Christmas, but I knew that wasn't happening. Chase and I both realized that we had some issues to work through first. I wasn't going to focus on that today. Today, I was going to celebrate Jesus, my family, and all of the good things that had happened in my life.

But there was a notable void in the fact that my dad wouldn't be here again. I wasn't sure when that would ever get easier.

"Holly," Chase called to me as the rest of the family disappeared into the living room.

I paused. "Yes?"

He held up a small brown bag with some crumpled red tissue paper sticking out from the top. "I want to give this to you in private."

I tilted my head, curious as to what could be inside. "Okay . . ."

I stepped closer and took the bag from him. Carefully, I pulled the tissue paper out. Whatever was inside, it was lightweight. My throat felt tight as I unfolded the supple paper and the gift cocooned in the middle was revealed.

Tears rushed to my eyes when I realized what it was. "It's beautiful."

I held up a wooden ornament. It was made in the shape of a heart, whittled from a soft wood. The letters "CD + HP 4-ever" were carved in the middle.

Chase squeezed my arm. "Do you like it?"

I brushed away some moisture from my cheeks. "It's beautiful. You made this?"

He nodded. "I don't know much about woodwork. But I remembered how much your father's ornaments meant to you, and I wanted to do something special. Believe it or not, that took me a couple of months. I threw several attempts away."

"It's perfect, Chase. I love it." I wrapped my arms around him, grateful for his thoughtfulness and the way he seemed to understand what made me tick.

I didn't want anything fancy or expensive. I cared more about people's hearts. And Chase couldn't have picked a more perfect present for me.

"You know you're special to me, Holly," he whispered in my ear.

I released my hold around his neck, settling back flat on my feet in order to see his eyes. My hand brushed his jaw. "I'm so glad God brought you into my life."

"I was wondering where you two went," Mom said, pausing in the foyer. "Sorry to interrupt."

"You're fine," I told her. I held up the ornament. "Look what Chase made me."

Her hand went over her heart. "Chase, that's gorgeous. Just perfect for Holly."

Chase grinned. "Good. I was a little nervous about it."

I squeezed his hand.

"You two do realize where you're standing, don't you?" my mom said.

I looked up and saw the mistletoe there.

I reached up and planted a soft kiss on Chase's lips.

Scrooge hadn't ruined our Christmas. No, gratitude had won.

###

If you enjoyed this book, you may also enjoy these other Holly Anna Paladin Mysteries:

***Random Acts of Murder* (Book 1)**
When Holly Anna Paladin is given a year to live, she embraces her final days doing what she loves most—random acts of kindness. But one of her extreme good deeds goes horribly wrong, implicating her in a string of murders. Holly is suddenly thrust into a different kind of fight for her life. Could it also be random that the detective assigned to the case is her old high school crush and present-day nemesis? Will Holly find the killer before he ruins what is left of her life? Or will she spend her final days alone and behind bars?

***Random Acts of Deceit* (Book 2)**
"Break up with Chase Dexter, or I'll kill him." Holly Anna Paladin never expected such a gut-wrenching ultimatum. With home invasions, hidden cameras, and bomb threats, Holly must make some serious choices. Whatever she decides, the consequences will either break her heart or break her soul. She tries to match wits with the Shadow Man, but the more she fights, the deeper she's drawn into the

perilous situation. With her sister's wedding problems and the riots in the city, Holly has nearly reached breaking point. She must stop this mystery man before someone she loves dies. But the deceit is threatening to pull her under . . . six feet under.

Random Acts of Malice (Book 3)
When Holly Anna Paladin's boyfriend, police detective Chase Dexter, says he's leaving for two weeks and can't give any details, she wants to trust him. But when she discovers Chase may be involved in some unwise and dangerous pursuits, she's compelled to intervene. Holly gets a run for her money as she's swept into the world of horseracing. The stakes turn deadly when a body surfaces and suspicion is cast on Chase. At every turn, more trouble emerges, making Holly question what she holds true about her relationship and her future. Just when she thinks she's on the homestretch, a dark horse arises. Holly might lose everything in a nail-biting fight to the finish.

Random Acts of Greed (Book 4)
Help me. Don't trust anyone. Do-gooder Holly Anna Paladin can't believe her eyes when a healthy baby boy is left on her doorstep. What seems like good fortune quickly turns into concern when blood spatter is found on the bottom of the baby carrier. Something tragic—

maybe deadly—happened in connection with the infant. The note left only adds to the confusion. What does it mean by "Don't trust anyone"? Holly is determined to figure out the identity of the baby. Is his mom someone from the inner-city youth center where she volunteers? Or maybe the connection is through Holly's former job as a social worker? Even worse— what if the blood belongs to the baby's mom? Every answer Holly uncovers only leads to more questions. A sticky web of intrigue captures her imagination until she's sure of only one thing: she must protect the baby at all cost.

Squeaky Clean Mysteries:

Hazardous Duty (Book 1)

On her way to completing a degree in forensic science, Gabby St. Claire drops out of school and starts her own crime-scene cleaning business. When a routine cleaning job uncovers a murder weapon the police overlooked, she realizes that the wrong person is in jail. But the owner of the weapon is a powerful foe . . . and willing to do anything to keep Gabby quiet. With the help of her new neighbor, Riley Thomas, a man whose life and faith fascinate her, Gabby seeks to find the killer before another murder occurs.

Suspicious Minds (Book 2)

In this smart and suspenseful sequel to *Hazardous Duty*, crime-scene cleaner Gabby St. Claire finds herself stuck doing mold remediation to pay the bills. Her first day on the job, she uncovers a surprise in the crawlspace of a dilapidated home: Elvis, dead as a doornail and still wearing his blue-suede shoes. How could she possibly keep her nose out of a case like this?

It Came Upon a Midnight Crime (Book 2.5, a Novella)

Someone is intent on destroying the true meaning of Christmas—at least, destroying anything that hints of it. All around crime-scene cleaner Gabby St. Claire's hometown, anything pointing to Jesus as "the reason for the season" is being sabotaged. The crimes become more twisted as dismembered body parts are found at the vandalisms. Someone is determined to destroy Christmas . . . but Gabby is just as determined to find the Grinch and let peace on earth and goodwill prevail.

Organized Grime (Book 3)
Gabby St. Claire knows her best friend, Sierra, isn't guilty of killing three people in what appears to be an eco-terrorist attack. But Sierra has disappeared, her only contact a frantic phone call to Gabby proclaiming she's being hunted. Gabby is determined to prove her friend is innocent and to keep Sierra alive. While trying to track down the real perpetrator, Gabby notices a disturbing trend at the crime scenes she's cleaning, one that ties random crimes together—and points to Sierra as the guilty party. Just what has her friend gotten herself involved in?

Dirty Deeds (Book 4)
"Promise me one thing. No snooping. Just for one week." Gabby St. Claire knows that her fiancé's request is a simple one she should be able to honor. After all, Riley's law school reunion and attorneys' conference at a posh resort is a chance for them to get away from the mysteries Gabby often finds herself involved in as a crime-scene cleaner. Then an old friend of Riley's goes missing. Gabby suspects one of Riley's buddies might be behind the disappearance. When the missing woman's mom asks Gabby for help, how can she say no?

The Scum of All Fears (Book 5)

Gabby St. Claire is back to crime-scene cleaning and needs help after a weekend killing spree fills her work docket. A serial killer her fiancé put behind bars has escaped. His last words to Riley were: *I'll get out, and I'll get even*. Pictures of Gabby are found in the man's prison cell, messages are left for Gabby at crime scenes, someone keeps slipping in and out of her apartment, and her temporary assistant disappears. The search for answers becomes darker when Gabby realizes she's dealing with a criminal who is truly the scum of the earth. He will do anything to make Gabby's and Riley's lives a living nightmare.

To Love, Honor, and Perish (Book 6)

Just when Gabby St. Claire's life is on the right track, the unthinkable happens. Her fiancé, Riley Thomas, is shot and in life-threatening condition only a week before their wedding. Gabby is determined to figure out who pulled the trigger, even if investigating puts her own life at risk. As she digs deeper into the case, she discovers secrets better left alone. Doubts arise in her mind, and the one man with answers lies on death's doorstep. Then an old foe returns and tests everything Gabby is made of—physically, mentally, and spiritually. Will all she's worked for be destroyed?

Mucky Streak (Book 7)

Gabby St. Claire feels her life is smeared with the stain of tragedy. She takes a short-term gig as a private investigator—a cold case that's eluded detectives for ten years. The mass murder of a wealthy family seems impossible to solve, but Gabby brings more clues to light. Add to the mix a flirtatious client, travels to an exciting new city, and some quirky—albeit temporary—new sidekicks, and things get complicated. With every new development, Gabby prays that her "mucky streak" will end and the future will become clear. Yet every answer she uncovers leads her closer to danger—both for her life and for her heart.

Foul Play (Book 8)

Gabby St. Claire is crying "foul play" in every sense of the phrase. When the crime-scene cleaner agrees to go undercover at a local community theater, she discovers more than backstage bickering, atrocious acting, and rotten writing. The female lead is dead, and an old classmate who has staked everything on the musical production's success is about to go under. In her dual role of investigator and star of the show, Gabby finds the stakes rising faster than the opening-night curtain. She must face her past and make monumental decisions, not just about the play but also concerning her future relationships and career. Will Gabby find the killer before the curtain goes down—not only on the play, but also on life as she knows it?

Broom and Gloom (Book 9)

Gabby St. Claire is determined to get back in the saddle again. While in Oklahoma for a forensic conference, she meets her soon-to-be stepbrother, Trace Ryan, an up-and-coming country singer. A woman he was dating has disappeared, and he suspects a crazy fan may be behind it. Gabby agrees to investigate, as she tries to juggle her conference, navigate being alone in a new place, and locate a woman who may not want to be found. She discovers that sometimes taking life by the horns means staring danger in the face, no matter the consequences.

Dust and Obey (Book 10)
When Gabby St. Claire's ex-fiancé, Riley Thomas, asks for her help in investigating a possible murder at a couples retreat, she knows she should say no. She knows she should run far, far away from the danger of both being around Riley and the crime. But her nosy instincts and determination take precedence over her logic. Gabby and Riley must work together to find the killer. In the process, they have to confront demons from their past and deal with their present relationship.

Thrill Squeaker (Book 11)
An abandoned theme park. An unsolved murder. A decision that will change Gabby's life forever. Restoring an old amusement park and turning it into a destination resort seems like a fun idea for former crime-scene cleaner Gabby St. Claire. The side job gives her the chance to spend time with her friends, something she's missed since beginning a new career. The job turns out to be more than Gabby bargained for when she finds a dead body on her first day. Add to the mix legends of

Bigfoot, creepy clowns, and ghostlike remnants of happier times at the park, and her stay begins to feel like a rollercoaster ride. Someone doesn't want the decrepit Mythical Falls to open again, but just how far is this person willing to go to ensure this venture fails? As the stakes rise and danger creeps closer, will Gabby be able to restore things in her own life that time has destroyed—including broken relationships? Or is her future closer to the fate of the doomed Mythical Falls?

Swept Away, a Honeymoon Novella (Book 11.5)
Finding the perfect place for a honeymoon, away from any potential danger or mystery, is challenging. But Gabby's longtime love and newly minted husband, Riley Thomas, has done it. He has found a location with a nonexistent crime rate, a mostly retired population, and plenty of opportunities for relaxation in the warm sun. Within minutes of the newlyweds' arrival, a convoy of vehicles pulls up to a nearby house, and their honeymoon oasis is destroyed like a sandcastle in a storm. Despite Gabby's and Riley's determination to keep to themselves, trouble comes knocking at their door—literally—when a neighbor is abducted from the beach directly outside their rental. Will Gabby and Riley be swept away with each other during their honeymoon . . . or will a tide of danger and mayhem pull them under?

Cunning Attractions (Book 12)
Politics. Love. Murder. Radio talk show host Bill

McCormick is in his prime. He's dating a supermodel, his book is a bestseller, and his ratings have skyrocketed during the heated election season. But when Bill's ex-wife, Emma Jean, turns up dead, the media and his detractors assume the opinionated loudmouth is guilty of her murder. Bill's on-air rants about his demon-possessed ex don't help his case. Did someone realize that Bill was the perfect scapegoat? Or could Bill have silenced his Ice Queen ex once and for all? Gabby Thomas takes on the case, but she soon realizes that Emma Jean had too many enemies to count. From election conspiracy theories to scorned affections and hidden secrets, Emma Jean left a trail of trouble as her legacy. Gabby is determined to follow the twisted path until she finds answers.

While You Were Sweeping, a Riley Thomas Novella
Riley Thomas is trying to come to terms with life after a traumatic brain injury turned his world upside down. Away from everything familiar—including his crime-scene-cleaning former fiancée and his career as a social-rights attorney—he's determined to prove himself and regain his old life. But when he claims he witnessed his neighbor shoot and kill someone, everyone thinks he's crazy. When all evidence of the crime disappears, even Riley has to wonder if he's losing his mind.

Note: _While You Were Sweeping_ is a spin-off mystery written in conjunction with the Squeaky Clean series featuring crime-scene cleaner Gabby St. Claire.

The Sierra Files:

Pounced (Book 1)

Animal-rights activist Sierra Nakamura never expected to stumble upon the dead body of a coworker while filming a project nor get involved in the investigation. But when someone threatens to kill her cats unless she hands over the "information," she becomes more bristly than an angry feline. Making matters worse is the fact that her cats—and the investigation—are driving a wedge between her and her boyfriend, Chad. With every answer she uncovers, old hurts rise to the surface and test her beliefs. Saving her cats might mean ruining everything else in her life. In the fight for survival, one thing is certain: either pounce or be pounced.

Hunted (Book 2)

Who knew a stray dog could cause so much trouble? Newlywed animal-rights activist Sierra Nakamura Davis must face her worst nightmare: breaking the news she eloped with Chad to her ultra-opinionated tiger mom. Her perfectionist parents have planned a vow-renewal ceremony at Sierra's lush childhood home, but a neighborhood dog ruins the rehearsal dinner when it shows up toting what appears to be a fresh human bone. While dealing with the dog, a nosy neighbor, and an old flame turning up at the wrong times, Sierra hunts for answers. Her journey of discovery leads to more than just who committed the crime.

Pranced (Book 2.5, a Christmas novella)

Sierra Nakamura Davis thinks spending Christmas with her husband's relatives will be a real Yuletide treat. But when the animal-rights activist learns his family has a reindeer farm, she begins to feel more like the Grinch. Even worse, when Sierra arrives, she discovers the reindeer are missing. Sierra fears the animals might be suffering a worse fate than being used for entertainment purposes. Can Sierra set aside her dogmatic opinions to help get the reindeer home in time for the holidays? Or will secrets tear the family apart and ruin Sierra's dream of the perfect Christmas?

Rattled (Book 3)

"What do you mean a thirteen-foot lavender albino ball python is missing?" Tough-as-nails Sierra Nakamura Davis isn't one to get flustered. But trying to balance being a wife and a new mom with her crusade to help animals is proving harder than she imagined. Add a missing python, a high maintenance intern, and a dead body to the mix, and Sierra becomes the definition of rattled. Can she balance it all—and solve a possible murder—without losing her mind?

The Worst Detective Ever:

Ready to Fumble
I'm not really a private detective. I just play one on TV.
Joey Darling, better known to the world as Raven
Remington, detective extraordinaire, is trying to
separate herself from her invincible alter ego. She
played the spunky character for five years on the hit TV
show Relentless, which catapulted her to fame and into
the role of Hollywood's sweetheart. When her marriage
falls apart, her finances dwindle to nothing, and her
father disappears, Joey finds herself on the Outer Banks
of North Carolina, trying to piece her life back together
away from the limelight. A woman finds Raven—er,
Joey—and insists on hiring her fictional counterpart to
find a missing boyfriend. When someone begins staging
crime scenes to match an episode of Relentless, Joey
has no choice but to get involved.

Reign of Error
Sometimes in life, you just want to yell "Take two!"
When a Polar Plunge goes terribly wrong and someone
dies in the icy water, former TV detective Joey Darling
wants nothing to do with subsequent investigation. But
when her picture is found in the dead man's wallet and
witnesses place her as the last person seen with the
man, she realizes she's been cast in a role she never
wanted: suspect. Joey makes the dramatic mistake of

CHRISTY BARRITT

challenging the killer on camera, and now it's a race to
find the bad guy before he finds her. Danger abounds
and suspects are harder to find than the Lost Colony of
Roanoke Island. But when Joey finds a connection with
this case and the disappearance of her father, she
knows there's no backing out. As hard as Joey tries to
be like her super detective alter ego, the more things go
wrong. Will Joey figure this one out? Or will her reign of
error continue?

Safety in Blunders
(coming soon)

Carolina Moon Series:

Home Before Dark (Book 1)

Nothing good ever happens after dark. Country singer Daleigh McDermott's father often repeated those words. Now, her father is dead. As she's about to flee back to Nashville, she finds his hidden journal with hints that his death was no accident. Mechanic Ryan Shields is the only one who seems to believe Daleigh. Her father trusted the man, but her attraction to Ryan scares her. She knows her life and career are back in Nashville and her time in the sleepy North Carolina town is only temporary. As Daleigh and Ryan work to unravel the mystery, it becomes obvious that someone wants them dead. They must rely on each other—and on God—if they hope to make it home before the darkness swallows them.

Gone By Dark (Book 2)

Ten years ago, Charity White's best friend, Andrea, was abducted as they walked home from school. A decade later, when Charity receives a mysterious letter that promises answers, she returns to North Carolina in search of closure. With the help of her new neighbor, Police Officer Joshua Haven, Charity begins to track down mysterious clues concerning her friend's abduction. They soon discover that they must work together or both of them will be swallowed by the looming darkness.

***Wait Until Dark* (Book 3)**

A woman grieving broken dreams. A man struggling to regain memories. A secret entrenched in folklore dating back two centuries. Antiquarian Felicity French has no clue the trouble she's inviting in when she rescues a man outside her grandma's old plantation house during a treacherous snowstorm. All she wants is to nurse her battered heart and wounded ego, as well as come to terms with her past. Now she's stuck inside with a stranger sporting an old bullet wound and forgotten hours. Coast Guardsman Brody Joyner can't remember why he was out in such perilous weather, how he injured his head, or how a strange key got into his pocket. He also has no idea why his pint-sized savior has such a huge chip on her shoulder. He has no choice but to make the best of things until the storm passes. Brody and Felicity's rocky start goes from tense to worse when danger closes in. Who else wants the mysterious key that somehow ended up in Brody's pocket? Why? The unlikely duo quickly becomes entrenched in an adventure of a lifetime, one that could have ties to local folklore and Felicity's ancestors. But sometimes the past leads to darkness . . . darkness that doesn't wait for anyone.

Light the Dark (a Christmas novella)
Nine months pregnant, Hope Solomon is on the run and fearing for her life. Desperate for warmth, food, and shelter, she finds what looks like an abandoned house.

Inside, she discovers a Christmas that's been left behind—complete with faded decorations on a brittle Christmas tree and dusty stockings filled with loss. Someone spies smoke coming from the chimney of the empty house and alerts Dr. Luke Griffin, the owner. He rarely visits the home that harbors so many bittersweet memories for him. But no one is going to violate the space so near and dear to his heart. Then Luke meets Hope, and he knows this mother-to-be desperately needs help. With no room at any local inn, Luke invites Hope to stay, unaware of the danger following her. While running from the darkness, the embers of Christmas present are stirred with an unexpected birth and a holiday romance. But will Hope and Luke live to see a Christmas future?

Cape Thomas Series:

Dubiosity (Book 1)

Savannah Harris vowed to leave behind her old life as an investigative reporter. But when two migrant workers go missing, her curiosity spikes. As more eerie incidents begin afflicting the area, each works to draw Savannah out of her seclusion and raise the stakes—for her and the surrounding community. Even as Savannah's new boarder, Clive Miller, makes her feel things she thought long forgotten, she suspects he's hiding something too, and he's not the only one. As secrets emerge and danger closes in, Savannah must choose between faith and uncertainty. One wrong decision might spell the end . . . not just for her but for everyone around her. Will she unravel the mystery in time, or will doubt get the best of her?

Disillusioned (Book 2)

Nikki Wright is desperate to help her brother, Bobby, who hasn't been the same since escaping from a detainment camp run by terrorists in Colombia. Rumor has it that he betrayed his navy brothers and conspired with those who held him hostage, and both the press and the military are hounding him for answers. All Nikki wants is to shield her brother so he has time to recover and heal. But soon they realize the paparazzi are the least of their worries. When a group of men try to abduct Nikki and her brother, Bobby insists that Kade

Wheaton, another former SEAL, can keep them out of harm's way. But can Nikki trust Kade? After all, the man who broke her heart eight years ago is anything but safe...Hiding out in a farmhouse on the Chesapeake Bay, Nikki finds her loyalties—and the remnants of her long-held faith—tested as she and Kade put aside their differences to keep Bobby's increasingly erratic behavior under wraps. But when Bobby disappears, Nikki will have to trust Kade completely if she wants to uncover the truth about a rumored conspiracy. Nikki's life—and the fate of the nation—depends on it.

Distorted (Book 3)
Coming soon

Standalones:

The Good Girl

Tara Lancaster can sing "Amazing Grace" in three harmonies, two languages, and interpret it for the hearing impaired. She can list the Bible canon backward, forward, and alphabetized. The only time she ever missed church was when she had pneumonia and her mom made her stay home. Then her life shatters and her reputation is left in ruins. She flees halfway across the country to dog-sit, but the quiet anonymity she needs isn't waiting at her sister's house. Instead, she finds a knife with a threatening message, a fame-hungry friend, a too-hunky neighbor, and evidence of . . . a ghost? Following all the rules has gotten her nowhere. And nothing she learned in Sunday School can tell her where to go from there.

Death of the Couch Potato's Wife (Suburban Sleuth Mysteries)

You haven't seen desperate until you've met Laura Berry, a career-oriented city slicker turned suburbanite housewife. Well-trained in the big-city commandment, "mind your own business," Laura is persuaded by her spunky seventy-year-old neighbor, Babe, to check on another neighbor who hasn't been seen in days. She finds Candace Flynn, wife of the infamous "Couch King," dead, and at last has a reason to get up in the morning. Someone is determined to stop her from digging deeper into the death of her neighbor, but Laura is just as determined to figure out who is behind the death-by-poisoned-pork-rinds.

Imperfect

Since the death of her fiancé two years ago, novelist Morgan Blake's life has been in a holding pattern. She has a major case of writer's block, and a book signing in the mountain town of Perfect sounds as perfect as its name. Her trip takes a wrong turn when she's involved in a hit-and-run: She hit a man, and he ran from the scene. Before fleeing, he mouthed the word "Help." First she must find him. In Perfect, she finds a small town that offers all she ever wanted. But is something sinister going on behind its cheery exterior? Was she invited as a guest of honor simply to do a book signing? Or was she lured to town for another purpose—a deadly purpose?

The Gabby St. Claire Diaries: a tween mystery series

The Curtain Call Caper (Book 1)

Is a ghost haunting the Oceanside Middle School auditorium? What else could explain the disasters surrounding the play—everything from missing scripts to a falling spotlight and damaged props? Seventh-grader Gabby St. Claire has dreamed about being part of her school's musical, but a series of unfortunate events threatens to shut down the production. While trying to uncover the culprit and save her fifteen minutes of fame, she also has to manage impossible teachers, cliques, her dysfunctional family, and a secret she can't tell even her best friend. Will Gabby figure out who or what is sabotaging the show . . . or will it be curtains for her and the rest of the cast?

The Disappearing Dog Dilemma (Book 2)

Why are dogs disappearing around town? When two friends ask seventh-grader Gabby St. Claire for her help in finding their missing canines, Gabby decides to unleash her sleuthing skills to sniff out whoever is behind the act. But time management and relationships get tricky as worrisome weather, a part-time job, and a new crush interfere with Gabby's investigation. Will her determination crack the case? Or will shadowy villains, a penchant for overcommitting, and even her own heart put her in the doghouse?

The Bungled Bike Burglaries (Book 3)

Stolen bikes and a long-forgotten time capsule leave one amateur sleuth baffled and busy. Seventh-grader Gabby St. Claire is determined to bring a bike burglar to justice—and not just because mean girl Donabell Bullock is strong-arming her. But each new clue brings its own set of trouble. As if that's not enough, Gabby finds evidence of a decades-old murder within the contents of the time capsule, but no one seems to take her seriously. As her investigation heats up, will Gabby's knack for being in the wrong place at the wrong time with the wrong people crack the case? Or will it prove hazardous to her health?

Complete Book List:

Squeaky Clean Mysteries:
#1 Hazardous Duty
#2 Suspicious Minds
#2.5 It Came Upon a Midnight Crime (a novella)
#3 Organized Grime
#4 Dirty Deeds
#5 The Scum of All Fears
#6 To Love, Honor, and Perish
#7 Mucky Streak
#8 Foul Play
#9 Broom and Gloom
#10 Dust and Obey
#11 Thrill Squeaker
#11.5 Swept Away (a novella)
#12 Cunning Attractions
#13 Clean Getaway (coming soon)

Squeaky Clean Companion Novella:
While You Were Sweeping

The Sierra Files:
#1 Pounced
#2 Hunted
#2.5 Pranced (a Christmas novella)
#3 Rattled
#4 Caged (coming soon)

RANDOM ACTS OF SCROOGE

The Gabby St. Claire Diaries (a Tween Mystery series):
#1 The Curtain Call Caper
#2 The Disappearing Dog Dilemma
#3 The Bungled Bike Burglaries

Holly Anna Paladin Mysteries:
#1 Random Acts of Murder
#2 Random Acts of Deceit
#3 Random Acts of Malice
#3.5 Random Acts of Scrooge
#4 Random Acts of Greed
#5 Random Acts of Fraud (coming soon)

The Worst Detective Ever:
#1 Ready to Fumble
#2 Reign of Error
#3 Safety in Blunders

Carolina Moon Series:
Home Before Dark
Gone By Dark
Wait Until Dark
Light the Dark (a Christmas novella)

Suburban Sleuth Mysteries:
#1 Death of the Couch Potato's Wife

Stand-alone Romantic-Suspense:
Keeping Guard
The Last Target

Race Against Time

Ricochet

Key Witness

Lifeline

High-Stakes Holiday Reunion

Desperate Measures

Hidden Agenda

Mountain Hideaway

Dark Harbor

Shadow of Suspicion

Cape Thomas Series:

Dubiosity

Disillusioned

Distorted (coming in 2017)

Standalone Romantic Mystery:

The Good Girl

Suspense:

Imperfect

Nonfiction:

Changed: True Stories of Finding God through Christian Music

The Novel in Me: The Beginner's Guide to Writing and Publishing a Novel

About the Author:

USA Today has called Christy Barritt's books "scary, funny, passionate, and quirky."

Christy writes both mystery and romantic suspense novels that are clean with underlying messages of faith. Her books have won the Daphne du Maurier Award for Excellence in Suspense and Mystery, have been twice nominated for the Romantic Times Reviewers' Choice Award, and have finaled for both a Carol Award and Foreword Magazine's Book of the Year.

She is married to her Prince Charming, a man who thinks she's hilarious—but only when she's not trying to be. Christy is a self-proclaimed klutz, an avid music lover who's known for spontaneously bursting into song, and a road trip aficionado.
When she's not working or spending time with her family, she enjoys singing, playing the guitar, and exploring small, unsuspecting towns where people have no idea how accident-prone she is.

Find Christy online at:
www.christybarritt.com
www.facebook.com/christybarritt
www.twitter.com/cbarritt

Sign up for Christy's newsletter to get information on all

of her latest releases here:
www.christybarritt.com/newsletter-sign-up/

If you enjoyed this book, please consider leaving a review.

RANDOM ACTS OF SCROOGE

Made in United States
Orlando, FL
12 December 2022

26342879R00096